J≠|C

S.M.U.R.K.

and the
Ozone Conspiracy

1

Margrit Cruickshank

*The first book in an exciting series
that just gets better and better!*

POOLBEG

To my family

First published 1990 by
Poolbeg Press Ltd,
123 Baldoyle Industrial Estate,
Dublin 13, Ireland
Reprinted 1992
This edition 1997

The Publishers gratefully acknowledge the support of The Arts Council.

A catalogue record for this book is available from the British Library.

ISBN 1 85371 212 4

Cover illustration by Leonard O'Grady
Cover design by Poolbeg Group Services Ltd
Printed and bound in Great Britain by
Cox & Wyman Ltd, Reading, Berks.

Contents

A Note on the Author

Award-winning author Margrit Cruickshank is perhaps best known for her popular S.K.U.N.K. series. *S.K.U.N.K. and the Ozone Conspiracy* was short-listed for the Irish Book Award in 1990. She was short-listed for the Bisto Book of the Year Award in 1991, and again in 1992, and was the winner of the 1993 Reading Association of Ireland Special Merit Book of the Year Award for her young adult novel, *Circling the Triangle*. *Anna's Six Wishes* was short-listed for a Children's Book Award in the UK in 1996 and is on their recommended reading list. Margrit Cruickshank lives and works in Dublin.

1
Seamus

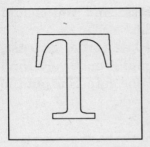he day that changed Aisling Daly's life started dull and miserable. Outside her bedroom window, the sea and sky merged in a single grey veil behind which Howth lay invisible. She groaned and dragged herself out of bed. Why ever had God created Mondays? He must have been mad.

By the time she got down to the kitchen, Kevin and her dad had already left for work. Her mother looked at the clock. "You'll be late again, Aisling. What on earth do you do with yourself in the mornings?"

"I meditate."

She dug her schoolbag out from under the pile of rubber boots, hockey sticks and coats in the hall, found her French book and propped it up against the milk bottle on the kitchen table.

1

She sat down opposite it and spread herself a piece of toast.

"You'll get indigestion," Mrs Daly said. "And spots. Breakfast should be a healthy, filling meal eaten in a relaxed mood with the minimum amount of stress. And you should have learnt that last night."

Aisling swallowed the last corner of toast, took a last look at the page of French verbs and drank her orange juice in one gulp. She put the book back in her bag.

"True," she admitted.

"What is?"

"Everything you say. I'll get indigestion and spots and I should have learnt that last night. How do you always manage to be so right?" She gave her mother a quick kiss. "Bye."

Mrs Daly smiled. "Bye, love. Don't forget to go round to Seamus after school."

"Mmm." Aisling grabbed her coat, slung her schoolbag over her shoulder and made for the door.

Her mother reached it before her. "I meant it," she said. "Be sure and go round."

"Oh, Mum! I can't! I told you I can't! I've hockey practice after school today. I can't miss it."

"You'll have to. You know Florence isn't

there on Mondays and someone has to see he gets his tea. I'm busy today, so it'll have to be you. I'm sorry, but that's how it is."

"He doesn't need anyone. You know he can make tea by himself if he has to. Florence just spoils him—and you're as bad. Please! I'll lose my place on the team if I miss another practice."

"He's a lonely, crippled old man, Aisling. And he's your godfather. I don't ask you often."

"I know, but—"

"No buts. Off you go, now, or you'll miss your bus." Mrs Daly opened the door. "Have a good day."

Fat chance, thought Aisling, as she ran to the bus stop. Double French, double Maths and Science—and now she'd have to skip hockey practice. Louise would probably get her place on the team, blast it. Unless—she cheered up: Louise might be sick again. There was a lot of 'flu about.

I'll have to start training properly, she told herself as the bus moved off. Maybe one day she'd be picked to play for Ireland. She imagined the headlines in the *Irish Times*: *Aisling Daly, our youngest international player, scored all six goals in last night's match against France.*

Blast Seamus, she thought.

***

Seamus O'Toole lived with his sister Florence in an old house overlooking Dalkey Hill. For as long as Aisling could remember, he had been confined to his bed, a huge bed with shiny brass rails at the head and the foot, and round brass balls on each corner. He was an inventor as well as an artist and his bedroom was a cross between a workshop, a studio and the laboratory of a mad scientist. One of his machines made cups of tea.

Aisling thought resentfully of this as she trudged up the hill from the bus stop. It was a long way and her schoolbag was heavy. And Louise was taking her place on the team for Saturday. It just wasn't fair.

She rang the bell.

"Yes?" grunted a voice through the grating by the door.

"It's me. Aisling."

"Hmm."

The door opened. Aisling left her bag in the hall and climbed upstairs. Seamus's studio would have to be in the attic. She wondered how Florence stood it.

As she reached the first landing, an orange ball which had been lying at the top of the second flight of stairs, just outside the studio door, uncurled itself and streaked down the stairs towards her. It crashed into her, nearly knocking her off balance, and twined round her ankles, purring like a pneumatic drill.

It was Mulligan, Florence's large marmalade cat.

She bent to pet him and he vibrated under her hand. As she went up the last flight of stairs he flew past her like a furry orange rocket and skidded to a halt on the polished linoleum at the top.

Aisling grinned. She knocked at the bedroom door.

"Come in!" roared a voice.

Aisling went in.

Seamus was sitting up in bed, gazing grumpily at a huge canvas attached to an easel in front of him. On either side of him, rows of buttons and knobs and switches were arranged like the instrument panel in an aircraft cockpit. These, Aisling knew, enabled him to do anything he needed—like open the front door or turn on the light or, she thought bitterly again, make cups of tea.

"Well?" he snorted.

Not really, thanks. Aisling bit back the retort. "Mum sent me," she said.

"Hmm."

"I'm to make your tea."

Seamus glared at her. "I have tea at 3 o'clock. It is now 4.18."

"I had to go to school."

"Rubbish! Nobody learns anything at school. You should have been here."

Aisling grinned. "It's the law," she explained. "I have to go to school."

"The law is an ass." Seamus frowned at the painting again. "Come over here."

Aisling edged her way round various bits of machinery to where she could see the canvas. Seamus had painted a country scene—a field of corn, a hedgerow, a stand of trees in the background. But everything was diseased: the corn was short and rust-coloured, the hedgerow stunted and ragged, the trees practically bare. She had never seen anything more depressing.

"Well?" Seamus snapped impatiently.

Aisling decided to be tactful. "It's...er...nice," she said.

"Nice!" Seamus exploded. "Art is not nice! Art is either good or bad, sublime or shoddy, but never nice!!"

"All right then. If you really want to know, it's awful."

"Hmm. Equally unanalytical, but at least honest. Why is it awful?"

"Everything looks sick." She looked at the

canvas more closely. "Yuck! There's a dead rabbit there and it's starting to rot. How could you?"

Seamus grinned at her. "You missed the nest of dead bluetits in the hedge and the magpie over on the left."

"It's gross!" Aisling was really upset. "I suppose you think you're being with-it and modern," she accused him. "Nobody wants that sort of sick art. What's wrong with a normal country scene—like whatsisname? The picture we have in the dining room? Paul Henry."

"Paul Henry!" Seamus snorted. "Our little grey home in the west!" He sighed. "It's true what they say: there's none so conservative as the young."

"You don't have to be conservative to like pretty things rather than sick ones."

"There you go again: pretty! Did nobody in school ever teach you Keats's Ode:
'Beauty is truth, truth beauty'—that is all
Ye know on earth, and all ye need to know.
No, obviously not. That painting, child, if Hermann is right, is the truth."

"Who's Hermann? One of these nutters who believes the end of the world is nigh?"

"Hermann is one of the greatest scientists of our age. And the end of the world may be nearer than you think. If what he believes is correct, we are in trouble."

"What sort of trouble?"

"Bad. Now, stop chattering for a moment and let me think."

"Me? Chattering?"

Seamus ignored her. He reached for a sketch pad and started to doodle thoughtfully.

Aisling stood up. She'd been told to visit Seamus. She'd visited Seamus who was in a foul mood and appeared to be going senile. Now she was going home. As she turned to leave, she banged her hand against one of his machines. "Ouch!"

"Now what?" Seamus looked up irritably.

"Nothing. I just bumped my hand."

"I just bumped my hand," Seamus mimicked. "Poor you."

"It hurt! We had an explosion in science today and I got cut by a bit of flying glass. It was a miracle nobody was seriously injured." So stop being so ruddy superior, she added to herself.

Seamus sat up. "An explosion?" he asked sharply. "What happened?"

"Mrs Healey was trying to show us that chlorine gas and hydrogen will mix—only she must have got it wrong because the whole thing exploded. Bang! There was glass everywhere and a whole lot of us got scratched or burnt by hydrochloric acid and the lab is a total disaster area. It wasn't funny, really. Nobody was badly hurt but poor Mrs Healey had to go away and lie down. Maybe she'll never be allowed to teach again."

"Now that is significant. Chlorine and hydrogen...Were you working near a flame—like a bunsen burner? Or could there have been a spark?"

"No. Even Mrs Healey's not that stupid."

"Hmm. Were you near an open window?"

"Well, yes."

"Hermann is right, then. It's as bad as he feared."

Before Aisling could decide whether to bother asking yet again who Hermann was and just what was as bad as he feared, the bell over the door jangled.

Seamus muttered something under his breath and reached for the speaking tube which hung above his bed. "Yes?"

Florence's voice came through the tube. "I'm back," she said. "Is Mary still there?"

"No. Aisling came instead. Late."

"I'll make you another pot of tea, so." There was a click and the tube went dead.

Seamus started to say something, thought better of it and pulled a lever at the other side of the bed. There was a creaking, clanking sound from the wall and a panel opened. A few minutes later the ropes in the lift shaft behind the panel moved and a trolley appeared. Seamus pressed another button and the trolley rolled out on to the carpet and trundled towards them.

It stopped beside Aisling. It was covered with a spotless lace-edged linen cloth. On top of this were two china cups with matching saucers and plates, a highly-polished silver teaset complete with water jug, milk jug and sugar bowl, and a plate of beautifully-cut anchovy sandwiches tastefully arranged on a paper doily. Aisling made a mental resolution that, next time she gave her parents breakfast in bed, she'd make more of an effort.

She poured the tea and placed a cup and the plate of anchovy sandwiches beside the bed. She helped herself to a sandwich and slipped it to Mulligan whose nose had emerged, twitching, from under the bed at the scent of food. Mulligan loved food: meat, fish, poultry, cheese, eggs, biscuits, chocolate, iced cakes and even hot roast chestnuts. It was one of the tragedies of his life that his main diet was tinned cat food.

"It's certainly very bad," said Seamus through a mouthful of sandwich. Aisling couldn't tell whether he was talking about the food or whatever it was that he'd been burbling on about earlier. She passed another sandwich to Mulligan.

"And if you think I don't know that you're feeding that animated food processor my favourite sandwiches, you're stupider than I thought."

Aisling blushed.

"I suppose I'll have to do as Hermann suggests. But first, I'd better check that it's still safe." He looked at her searchingly. "I can't go myself," he said. "So someone has to. And seeing you're here, you might as well. Can you keep a secret?"

"Yes," said Aisling. "I think so."

"Thinking's not enough."

"Well, I know so, then."

"Can you prove it?"

Aisling hesitated. "Well... I never told anyone about Kevin's..." She stopped.

"Good enough," said Seamus. "Now, listen carefully. You know the portrait of Synge?"

"Who?"

"Synge. John Millington Synge. Playwright.

*The Playboy of the Western World. Riders to the
Sea.* What do they teach you in school
nowadays?"

"No," said Aisling. "I don't. Is it in town
somewhere?"

"In the Municipal Gallery in Parnell Square.
It's painted by John B Yeats, in case you're
interested. Not that you would be. The father of
William Butler Yeats. I take it you've heard of
him?"

"*I will arise and go now and go to Innisfree...*"
Aisling quoted wearily. "We had to learn it at
school."

"You surprise me."

"Anyway, what's that got to do with
Hermann, whoever he is, and his problem?"

"There's a copy of the portrait downstairs in
the parlour. Above the mantelpiece."

Aisling had been in the parlour once, looking
for something with Florence. She remembered
a dim, high-ceilinged room full of dark, heavy
furniture, smelling of dust and stale air. "What
about it?" she asked.

Seamus closed his eyes and Aisling
wondered for a moment if he'd gone to sleep.
Then: "I think that's right. Now. Pay attention.
When you look at the mantelpiece, you'll see a
lady with a figure like an elephant's behind on

the right side of the fireplace. She's holding something which the sculptor, bless his innocent soul, obviously thought was a Greek vase. One of the objects in the vase works the secret panel."

Aisling whistled. "Brill! Which one?"

"I can't remember." He chuckled. "That interests you at last. I only hope it hasn't interested someone else. I want you to take down the picture, open the panel and bring me what you find in it. Be very careful with it. It's..."

CRASH!!!

There was a noise of breaking glass and a figure plunged through the skylight.

2
The Window Cleaner

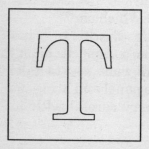he intruder smashed through the network of wires and tubes crisscrossing the ceiling, missed the easel by inches and landed in a heap on the carpet. Mulligan bolted back under the bed. The speaking tube whistled urgently. "What's going on up there?" demanded Florence.

Seamus reached over for the tube. "I haven't the slightest idea. Why don't you come up and see for yourself? And get your crossbow out of the airing cupboard—it might be needed." Aisling looked at him in surprise: for the first time since she'd arrived, he actually sounded happy.

"Bring a dustpan and brush up too," he added, looking at the mess on the floor.

The intruder sat up slowly. He stretched out

his arms gingerly, wriggled his toes, rubbed the back of his neck, went ouch! and removed a piece of glass from the seat of his trousers and stood up.

"Stay where you are!" warned a voice from the doorway. "Don't move or I'll shoot."

The man turned slowly. Aisling stared.

Florence stood in the doorway. She was a little woman, her kindly pink face was framed by a halo of white sausage-like curls, her sleeves were rolled up, her arms covered in flour, her short plump form was enveloped in a pink floral pinny—and in her hands was a wicked-looking crossbow, loaded and aimed at the intruder.

He put his hands on his head. "Jaysus! Don't shoot, Missus! Sure, I was only doing me job. It's not my fault the window's busted, honest it isn't. I was just cleaning it and it fell in on me. Them ould windows should be replaced, sure they should. I could sue, like—" He caught Florence's eye. "—only I won't say another word about it. I'll just go now and get on with the ones downstairs."

Florence didn't move. "I never asked to have my windows cleaned."

"Sure you did." The man tried a weasely grin and then thought better of it. "This is number five, isn't it?"

"No."

"Ah, there you have it then, Missus. Sure, himself has sent me to the wrong house. I'll just be getting out of your way now, if you'll move that weapon there a teeny bit..."

Florence turned to Aisling. "Go down to the kitchen and fetch the dustpan and brush—your godfather obviously imagines I have three hands. As for you, my man," she said to the intruder, "I shall have a word with your employer."

"Don't do that, Missus," he whined. "You'll get me the sack, sure you will. And what'll me kids and the ould wan do then?"

"Poor things," added Aisling automatically, thinking of the nursery rhyme.

Florence threw her a disapproving glance. "I thought I told you to fetch the dustpan?"

Aisling raced down to the kitchen, muttering under her breath. Hockey practice would have been a rest cure compared to all this running up and down stairs. She grabbed the dustpan and raced back up again. Everyone was still where they'd been before: Florence with the crossbow, the man with his hands on his head and Seamus in bed with a delighted grin on his face.

"Take the dustpan from the child and clean

up that mess—properly," ordered Florence. "And then you can give me the name and address of your employer. And don't ever come back here again."

The man got down on his knees and started sweeping up the glass and broken metal. "I couldn't do that, Missus, sure I couldn't. I'm self-employed, like."

Florence looked at him. "How many children did you say you had?" she asked abruptly. "And there's a bit of glass over there that you missed—under the table," she added.

The man hesitated. "Sixteen," he said and crawled obediently under the table.

"Hmm."

"Well... To be honest with you, Missus, only twelve alive," he amended hastily. "There's four in Heaven, God rest them." He blessed himself and wiped a hand across his eyes.

Florence's expression softened. She made an attempt to look stern again. "I don't know if I altogether believe you, but the insurance company will no doubt pay for the window so we'll forget about it this time."

"God bless you, Missus," whined the man. "I'll say a prayer for you."

"Leave Him out of it. Look into the kitchen on the way out and I'll give you some scones for the children." Florence handed her crossbow to Seamus, glared at him as if daring him to say anything, and left.

The man put down the dustpan and started to follow.

"Oh no you don't!" roared Seamus, pointing the crossbow at him.

The man stopped in his tracks and turned round.

"Lock the door, Aisling, and give me the key." Aisling did so.

"Now. What were you doing on my roof?"

"Sure, amn't I just after telling you? I was washing the windows," whined the man with an air of injured innocence. "You heard the lady."

"My daughter would believe every scoundrel with a sob story from here to Donegal. I am less credulous. Who sent you?"

"Nobody. I told you, I work on me own, like."

Seamus looked at him hard. "Was it S.K.U.N.K.?" he asked quietly.

The man jumped. Aisling could have sworn his pasty complexion turned even paler. She wondered who or what S.K.U.N.K. was— obviously something important."

"I don't know what you're talking about, Mister," the man said hurriedly. "I'm off." He moved towards the door. "Hey," he said, turning the handle. "You've no right to do that! You let me out of here, see."

"Or you'll call the police?" suggested Seamus. "That'd be the day. Just you answer my questions and then you can leave. Why were you spying on me?"

Aisling turned to stare at her godfather. Was he out of his mind? Why should anyone spy on him, of all people? Or did it have something to do with Hermann, whoever he was, and whatever was behind the secret panel? She looked back at the window cleaner, hoping for an explanation.

"Me? Spying on you? You've been reading too many thrillers, Mister." And yet the man's laugh sounded forced.

Seamus sighed. "Have it your own way, then." He threw Aisling the key. "Let him out. I doubt if he can tell us much, in any case."

Aisling unlocked the door and the man rushed towards it. As he was leaving, Seamus called after him. "Tell S.K.U.N.K. we'll fight," he said. "They won't get away with it."

The man turned round. He straightened his back and, abandoning the whining tone he had used with Florence, sneered openly. "Fight, is it? Sure, you're too old, Grandad. Just keep out of this, if you know what's good for you. We'll be watching you and, if you make one move to contact your friends..." The man's weasely face assumed on an expression of such hate and cruelty that Aisling took a step nearer Seamus's bed.

Seamus remained unmoved. "Oh, get out," he said wearily.

"Sure, Grandad. But you can't say you haven't been warned." The man glared at them both and slammed the door behind him.

"Make sure he leaves the house," Seamus ordered Aisling.

She watched from the landing as the intruder sauntered down to the kitchen, accepted a huge carrier bag of food from Florence and went out into the street. "What was all that about?" she asked as she got back to the studio. "Who's S.K.U.N.K.? And what's going on?"

"S.K.U.N.K. is as nasty a bunch of central European gentlemen as you are ever likely to meet. You could say the letters stand for Skulduggery, Killing, Unscrupulousness, Nastiness and Corruption. They are out to gain world power—if they do, God help us. At least Hermann's ahead of them this time, but we'll have to work fast. And first, I'd better see just how bad things are. Put this damn firearm

away somewhere and pass me my dressing
gown from the wardrobe—it's draughty with
that hole in the skylight. And then go down and
bring up what you find in the safe."

"I won't," said Aisling. "Not until you tell me
what's happening."

Seamus looked at her coolly for a minute. "All
right," he said. "I'll ask Florence." He reached
for the speaking tube.

"Please!"

"Are you going to open that safe or aren't you?
I haven't got all day."

Aisling gave in. "You win."

3
Experiments

isling entered the parlour in a state of suppressed excitement: *Special agent Aisling Daly finds vital plans behind secret panel...*

The curtains were closed to protect the furniture from the sunlight. As she opened them, something in the road beyond the front hedge caught her eye. It had been like the flash of sun on a mirror—or from the windscreen of a moving car. She looked: there was a red car parked on the road, half-hidden by the hedge. Could somebody have been watching the house through binoculars?

She grinned to herself; she was becoming as bad as Seamus! All the same, she closed the curtains again and put on the light. There was no point in taking chances.

The fireplace was exactly as Seamus had described it. She pressed the fruit in the basket carried by the marble lady, but nothing happened. Then she tried turning them. The third one moved. The picture of Synge above the mantelpiece tilted through an angle of forty-five degrees until it pointed straight at a flight of china ducks on the window wall. She unhooked the portrait: behind it, a hole had appeared. Standing on tiptoe on the brass fender, she felt inside the hole. Her fingers touched something!

She drew it out and looked at it. It was a small metal box. She tried to open it but it was locked. She tested the weight of it in her hand. It was very heavy for something so small. She remembered hearing that gold was one of the heaviest metals. Could it contain a bar of gold? *Schoolgirl becomes millionaire overnight!* She rushed back upstairs.

"Can I open it?"

Seamus took the box from her and examined it carefully. "It doesn't look as if anyone's been tampering with it but we'd better check, just to make sure."

Taking a key from a drawer beside his bed, he unlocked the box. Aisling waited breathlessly. Louise would never believe her!

Seamus opened the lid. To Aisling's disappointment, the box contained nothing more exciting than a small compact machine, full of knobs and dials and bits of wires.

"What on earth's that?" she asked.

"A component."

"A what?"

"An integral part of a greater whole."

Seamus gave an infuriating smile. He was obviously waiting for her to ask what that meant. She wasn't going to oblige him. "What does it do?" she asked instead.

"By itself, nothing. But if the machine of which it is a part does what we hope it will do, we might save the world yet."

"You keep on about the world. Save it from what?"

Seamus seemed to change the subject. "I don't suppose they teach you anything about the ozone layer at that school of yours, do they?"

"Naturally." Aisling grinned. They'd just had a geography test on pollution and for once, she could actually get one up on her godfather. "It's a layer of the upper atmosphere, about six to thirty miles above the earth's surface. It absorbs ultra-violet radiation from the sun, thus protecting the earth's atmosphere. They discovered a hole in it at the south pole some time ago, and another at the north pole quite recently. If we don't do something, like ban aerosols and gases in refrigerators and plastic foam and things, we'll all get skin cancer and die." She groaned. "I can't even sunbathe these days without Mum coming rushing out with a bottle of suntan oil just in case."

"I am impressed." Seamus didn't sound it. "It's not just skin cancer, however. Ultra-violet light harms all living cells, in plants as well as in animals. If we don't all die of cancer, we'll die of starvation."

"Charming."

"Yes. S.K.U.N.K. has really come up with a nice idea this time."

"S.K.U.N.K? That gang you were talking about? What have they to do with the ozone layer? I thought it was the gases from aerosols and things, C.F.C.s or whatever they're called..."

"Chlorofluorocarbons."

"Whatever, that are making the holes."

"They are. At the poles. If Hermann is right, this particular hole is over Europe."

"It's *what?* How do you know that? There hasn't been anything about it on the telly."

"There hasn't been anything about it on the telly," Seamus mimicked. "And if it's not on the telly, it doesn't exist. How convenient for you."

"All right. How do you know there's a hole in the ozone layer up there?" Aisling pointed up through the broken skylight.

"That explosion in your science class. Unless they're exposed to a spark or a flame, hydrogen and chlorine gas only explode if you shine ultra-violet light on them."

"And it's ultra-violet light that gives us skin cancer! Why didn't Mrs Healey think of that?"

"Holes in the ozone layer are not the first thing most people think about when an accident happens," Seamus remarked drily. "I probably wouldn't have thought of it myself, if I hadn't been warned. There's another test we can make, though. Look in the bottom drawer over there. There should be a Polaroid camera somebody gave me once. I think it's still got film in it."

Aisling found the camera snuggling under a pile of garish ties, socks, cigarette lighters and bottles of after-shave: obviously years of unwanted Christmas presents. She recognised some of the socks and one particular brand of after-shave. She'd know better this Christmas.

"All right. Now, go downstairs and take a few photographs."

"Of anything in particular?"

"No. Just get a move on, child. I haven't got all day."

Aisling bit back a retort and went down stairs again. If she had to do much more of this, she thought grimly, she could skip fitness training this week with a good conscience.

She took a photo of Dalkey Hill and waited for it to develop. It was all fuzzy. She took another. Still fuzzy. She tried a third photo, this time of the house. The result was the same. The camera must be bust, she thought. Seamus will be delighted.

She climbed back up the three flights of stairs to the studio.

"You're unfit," Seamus said.

She ignored him. "The camera's broken. And before you say anything, it wasn't my fault. I didn't do anything."

"Was I going to say anything? Did it take any pictures at all."

"Well, yes. But they're all foggy. And I didn't shake the camera. I was very careful."

Seamus looked at the photographs. "I believe you. That haze is not from shaking the camera. That is ultra-violet light interfering with the optics. You get the same problem up in the mountains, which is why photographers use a UV-rejecting filter in high altitudes. It certainly shouldn't happen down here. There must be a lot of ultra-violet out there... Let's try an experiment to find out."

He rummaged in one of the drawers of the cabinet beside his bed. "There should be some quartz lenses here... Yes. Fine. Pass me that prism over there, Aisling, please. You do know what a prism is, I suppose?"

Aisling didn't bother to answer him. She picked up the triangular piece of heavy crystal, shaped like a bar of Toblerone chocolate, which was acting as a paper-weight on top of a pile of sketches, and handed it to him.

He took a gadget out of another drawer.

"What's that?" Aisling asked.

"I need to pass light from an electric spark through the quartz lenses. This machine will give me the spark. Now..." He placed a piece of white sketching paper under the prism. "I don't know if this will work, but we can try. Pull the blind across the skylight a bit, will you?"

Aisling pulled the blind cord. The blind came half-way across the skylight and then jammed on the broken frame.

"Don't worry. That should be dark enough. Now... watch!"

He pressed the switch on the electrical gadget. There was a bright spark.

Aisling, staring at the white sheet of paper, saw the colours of the spectrum reflected onto it through the prism.

"Well?" Seamus asked.

"Roy G Biv."

"I beg your pardon?"

"Roy G Biv: the colours of the spectrum. Red, orange, yellow, green, blue, indigo, violet. Same as a rainbow."

"You don't say. Now, will you stop showing off and tell me what you *see* instead of what you *think* you see. Look carefully at the blue end of the spectrum. I'll pass a spark through again."

Aisling looked. The spectrum spread over the paper again. It was just the same as the spectrum they'd created in an experiment in school, only... It extended out beyond the violet bar! "Is that ultra-violet light?" she asked in amazement."

"Indeed it is." Seamus sounded grave. "And it's stronger than I had thought. S.K.U.N.K. have really excelled themselves this time. We'll have to act quickly."

"What have S.K.U.N.K. done?" Aisling asked again. "And why?"

"Not to mention when? and where?" Seamus mocked. "Stop wasting my time, child. I have to get moving. There's a travel agent down in

Dalkey, isn't there? You'd better go down there
now and get tickets."

Aisling looked at her watch: it was just 6 p.m.
"They'll be closed," she said. "And please won't
you tell me what's going on?"

"Closed!" Seamus snorted. "No wonder the
country's in the mess it is. In that case, you'd
better go home now. I have a lot of things to do."
He reached for the speaking tube. "Florence!
Come up here! We're going to Switzerland!"

"Switzerland!" Aisling looked at him in
amazement.

"I thought I told you to go home." Seamus
replaced the machine Aisling had found in the
parlour back in its box.

"But—"

"Out!" He put the box under his pillow and
reached for his sketch pad.

"It's not fair. I promise I won't tell anyone."

"Are you going?" Seamus picked up a heavy
book from the table and aimed it at her.

"Rats," she said. And left.

4
S.K.U.N.K.

isling stopped at the front door and looked round, trying to see some evidence of a hole in the sky up above her.

The whole thing's mad, she thought. To heck with Seamus and his complicated experiments: his camera obviously wasn't working properly and the explosion at school had just been a bit of bad luck. Seamus was getting on; he could easily have started to go senile and be imagining things. People did when they were old, she told herself firmly. He was beginning to get paranoid, too, thinking people were after him. She must have been crazy even to have listened to him. Slinging her schoolbag over her shoulder, she started to walk down towards Dalkey.

Suddenly she heard a car engine start up behind her. She turned. The red car which had been parked near Seamus's house pulled out from the kerb and came towards her. She'd forgotten all about it. Now she remembered that the window cleaner had threatened that they'd be watching —whoever they were. She walked faster.

The car drew up alongside her and a door opened. She dropped her schoolbag and ran. Someone got out of the car and followed her. She could hear footsteps pounding on the pavement behind her, getting closer and closer. There was a house just ahead, she remembered. If she could only reach it, she'd knock at the door and ask them to call the police. She just had to stay ahead of the man behind her.

Then the car passed her again. It stopped between her and the house. A small thin man got out and stood on the pavement, waiting for her.

She swerved and ran across the road. Without thinking, she headed up the hill towards Dalkey quarry. The grass deadened the sound of her pursuers' footsteps, but she didn't dare turn round to see how close they were.

Ahead of her, the trees round the quarry

loomed out of the evening mist. Panic hit her. Of all the stupid places to come! They could murder her here and there would be nobody to notice.

She veered right and headed for the car park. Maybe someone would be walking their dog. Yes—there was a sports car parked at the side of the road. She made a last effort and ran towards it, thinking her heart would burst.

The car door opened and a man got out. He came towards her and caught her as she fell into his arms.

"It's Aisling, isn't it? Seamus's god-daughter? I didn't expect to bump into you like this!" He held her away from him and looked her up and down. "Mind you, although I'm all in favour of keeping fit, don't you think you're overdoing it? Especially at this time of the evening?"

Aisling stared at him, open-mouthed. He was middle-aged and stoutish, with thinning fair hair and a cheerful face, and he was smiling down at her as if she was a long-lost daughter: yet she could swear she had never seen him before in her life.

She looked round. Two men were standing in the grass a few yards away, watching them. One was big and swarthy and looked like a gorilla in the gathering dusk; the other was small and thin.

The middle-aged man followed her gaze. "Aha," he said. "Laurel and Hardy. Are they friends of yours?"

"No," said Aisling vehemently.

"Ah, well then. In that case we'll bid them adieu." He raised his hat to the two men, grasped Aisling by the arm, opened the car door, thrust her into the passenger's seat, leapt agilely round the front of the bonnet and into the driver's seat and drove off. Before Aisling realized what was happening, they were roaring towards Killiney village.

She had been kidnapped!

The man smiled at her, looking almost boyish. "Are Laurel and Hardy still with us?" he asked.

Aisling turned in her seat. The red car was racing along the road behind them.

"Ah yes," said the plumpish man. "So they are. Tighten your seatbelts, ladies and gentlemen, and prepare for take-off."

He put his foot down hard on the accelerator and the sports car shot forwards. Aisling watched the speedometer needle reach 40, then 50, then 60 m.p.h. as they sped up the narrow road past Killiney Park Gates. Fortunately, there was no other traffic.

She glanced at the man beside her. He was hunched forwards in his seat, grinning impishly as he concentrated on guiding the car round the bends. She imagined the headlines in the paper: *Schoolgirl abducted by maniac. The body of Aisling Daly, one of Ireland's most promising hockey players, was found yesterday on Killiney Hill...*

Her mother had always warned her about accepting lifts from strange men. Not that there'd been much chance of refusing...

She looked behind again. The red car was still following.

"Don't worry," said the plumpish man. "We'll easily lose them."

He turned sharply to the right at Killiney village and then swerved, his tyres screeching, into one of the tiny roads on the left. Aisling closed her eyes and held her breath as they tore down a series of back lanes.

"Okay. You can breathe again now." The plumpish man patted her arm encouragingly. She moved away quickly and opened her eyes.

They were down in Dalkey village, driving at a sedate 30 m.p.h. She looked behind: there was no sign of the red car. "Thanks," she said. "You can drop me off here."

She wasn't really surprised when the man shook his head. "Not at all. I'll drive you home."

Aisling forced herself to smile. She had a better chance of escaping, she calculated, if he thought she trusted him.

They had to slow down for traffic in the centre of Dalkey and Aisling saw her chance. She opened the car door and was out like a flash, before he had time to grab her back. She darted into a newsagent's shop; at least, if he followed her in there, someone would help or call the police. She waited for what seemed like hours, scared to look out in case he was waiting for her. At last the shop assistant lost patience: "Well? Are you going to buy anything?"

She found some money in her pocket and bought a chocolate bar. The plumpish man still hadn't appeared. Keeping well back behind a soft-ice machine, she peered into the street. The sports car had gone.

Feeling like someone in a detective film, Aisling sidled out of the shop. She looked up and down the pavement in case he was hiding somewhere, waiting for her to come into the open again: there was no sign of him. She walked close behind a couple of elderly ladies towards the bus stop: still no sign. It was only when she reached her own front door that she allowed herself to relax.

She let herself into the house.

"Is that you, Aisling?" Her mother was in the front room.

No, it's a gang of thugs come to murder you, she thought. She controlled herself. "Yes, Mum."

Mrs Daly came into the kitchen and sat on a stool by the table. Aisling would rather have been left alone. She needed to think.

"Your tea's in the oven. We ate early. Your father had to go to a meeting of the Neighbourhood Watch committee and Kevin's out with Sally—as usual."

"Mmm."

"How was Seamus then?"

"Fine."

"Did Florence get back before you left?"

"Mmm." Aisling speared a piece of sausage and carefully balanced a dollop of mashed potato and six baked beans on top of it.

Her mother shrugged slightly and smiled, more at herself than at Aisling. "Have you a lot of homework?"

Aisling suddenly remembered that she'd dropped her schoolbag when the men from the red car had chased her. It must still be outside Seamus's house. "Rats," she said.

Her mother raised an eyebrow.

"I left my bag at Seamus's. It's okay. I'll get up early tomorrow and cycle up before school. We don't have much homework and I can do it at break, anyway."

"You'll forget yourself, one day." Her mother sighed and stood up. "Clear up when you've finished, then. And you'd better get to bed early—you'll have to be up by seven tomorrow."

"Mum?" Aisling looked up.

"Yes?"

"Does Dad have a sort of fattish, balding, middle-aged friend who drives a black sports car?"

Mrs Daly thought for a minute. "No. Not that I can think of. Though I don't know all his friends, naturally. Why?"

"Oh, nothing." Aisling took another mouthful of supper. "Do you know a friend of Seamus's called Hermann? Or an organisation called S.K.U.N.K.?"

Her mother looked at her suspiciously. "No. What's all this about?"

"Nothing," said Aisling. "I just wondered."

There was a ring at the door. Mrs Daly gave Aisling a worried look and went to answer it. Aisling heard her open the door.

"I'm sorry," she heard her say. "We don't

want any."

A voice muttered something Aisling couldn't make out.

"I don't wish to see them. I told you, I'm not interested. What—?"

Aisling looked round the corner of the door. Her mouth fell open. A middle-aged, plumpish, balding man had just edged his way past her mother into the hall. It was the owner of the black sports car.

She came slowly out of the kitchen. The man held a battered briefcase and was obviously posing as a door-to-door salesman. Who on earth was he?

"Shall I call Kevin?" she asked her mother.

"By all means call Kevin," said the man cheerfully. "The more the merrier. Who's Kevin?"

"My brother. And he's over six foot and he weighs fourteen stone and he's a fifth Dan at karate." Whoever the man was, Aisling thought, that ought to get rid of him.

"Is he interested in improving his mind, though?" asked the plumpish man. "That is the question. And you yourself, young lady, you strike me as being the sort of intelligent young woman who is only waiting to acquire a hand-crafted, machine-tooled, imitation-leather edition of the *Encyclopedia for the Expansion of Young Minds* in order to realise your already considerable potential for intellectual excellence. As it happens, I have an example here."

He seemed completely unaware of the icy atmosphere around him. As he struggled with the clasp of his briefcase, Mrs Daly tried again to push him out. "Please don't bother," she said. "We're really not interested. And besides, we can't afford it."

"Ah," said the plumpish man with an even cheerier smile. "But that is only because I haven't told you about our Easy Payment Plan. Anybody can afford an *Encyclopedia for the Expansion of Young Minds*; but who can afford not to buy one? I ask you!" His hand paused above the second lock. Aisling watched anxiously. Her hope that Seamus was imagining things had been shattered by the car chase up on Dalkey Hill. Someone was obviously out to get him and anybody connected with him. This man could be one of the enemy too. Goodness knows what his briefcase contained. A bomb, a gun, poison gas— anything was possible. *Mystery deaths in South County Dublin!* she thought.

She edged along the hall, hoping to get close

enough to tackle him and push him outside before the second lock opened. Fortunately, the man wasn't looking at her. He was gazing at Mrs Daly with an expression of admiration on his face. "I can see you're an intelligent woman," he said. "You wouldn't want to deny your children this unique opportunity of improving their minds. It's hard times we live in..." He sighed theatrically. "In the rat race for jobs, every advantage counts."

The second clasp gave. Aisling dived. Mrs Daly shut the door. All at the same time.

The salesman helped Aisling to her feet. "There you are, now," he said to Mrs Daly. "I told you she was a girl of initiative and decision. Your sitting room is through here, isn't it?" He pushed open the front room door. "One never feels really at ease, chatting in halls and doorways, does one? Won't you sit down?"

"I thought I had made it clear," said Mrs Daly coldly, "that I have no wish to buy your encyclopedia. Will you please leave my house."

"Ah, but of course you haven't," said the salesman agreeably. "How could you? You haven't seen it yet. Here, let me show you Volume 10—it covers the letters S and T."

He took a dull red volume from his briefcase and opened it. "There," he said. "Switzerland."

Aisling jumped. He appeared not to notice. "Two whole pages. Tells you everything you could ever wish to know. I ask you, Madam, just look for yourself."

"I already know all I want to know about Switzerland," said Mrs Daly even more coldly.

"Did you know that its mountains rise to a height of 14,688 feet?" asked the salesman imperturbably, reading from the book. "And that..." he turned a page, "it plays host to various international organisations like the United Nations and the Red Cross and S.K.U.N.K.?" Aisling drew in her breath sharply. "It also," he went on, "produces clocks, chocolates, cheese, chemicals..."

"And," interrupted Mrs Daly, "its citizens believe in democracy and law-and-order and would no doubt put people like you who push themselves uninvited into other people's houses into jail. For the last time, will you please leave?"

The salesman looked pained. "Perhaps Switzerland was the wrong example," he said hurriedly. "Let's try T. Tarantulas, Television, Thinning of the ozone layer... I'll bet you don't know anything about that."

"Aisling, will you please ring the police."

Aisling picked up the phone.

"No need, no need," said the salesman. "I can see when I'm not wanted. I shall leave you this volume. Keep it for ten days on free trial and then you can send it back to me if you can still resist it. Perhaps Aisling's godfather would like to look at it." Before either of them could say anything, he had shut his briefcase, raised his hat politely and left.

"Thank goodness for that," said Mrs Daly, slamming the door behind him. "I thought we'd never get rid of him. Why, Aisling, what's the matter? You look very pale."

Aisling pulled herself together. "I've got a headache, Mum. I'll be okay. I'll take an aspirin and go right to bed. As you said, I have to be up early tomorrow."

Once in her bedroom, she sat down on her bed and started to open the encyclopedia she'd been left. Then she put it down quickly. It could be a disguised bomb! He'd told her to show it to Seamus. Maybe that was how they meant to stop him doing whatever it was he had to do!

She looked it anxiously. Should she call the bomb squad? Rats, she thought. I'm getting as bad as Seamus. It's nothing but a plain, ordinary book. Your man had it open downstairs and nothing happened. Gingerly she turned back the cover with the end of a ruler. The book didn't explode. She flicked a few pages over. Still nothing happened.

She picked the book up and looked through it. It was just an ordinary volume of an ordinary encyclopedia. The entry under Switzerland was quite normal. It mentioned all the things he had said it did. Except S.K.U.N.K. And there was nothing about the ozone layer at all. She looked for Ultra-violet, just in case, but the volume only dealt with S and T.

She heard her father come in. He was the street organiser for the Neighbourhood Watch scheme. Kevin and Aisling had tried to convince him that, with Mrs Hegarty living opposite and looking out of her windows all day long, it was quite unnecessary on their street, but they hadn't succeeded. She wondered if Mrs Hegarty had seen the encyclopedia salesman.

Who on earth was he? If he was one of the enemy, why had he rescued her from the two men in the red car? And if he wasn't, why had he come to her house, pretending to sell encyclopedias? How did he know where she lived? Not only that, how had he known her name at Dalkey Hill? And above all, why had he left her a volume of his encyclopedia?

***

It was a long time before she got to sleep. And when she did, she dreamt that she was ski-ing down a mountain with an encyclopedia under her arm and the salesman at her side, urging her to buy the full, luxury edition for only £14,688. Behind them, gaining fast, were the two men from the red car: they were wearing bowler hats above their anoraks and looked more like Laurel and Hardy than ever. Suddenly there was a prism-shaped tree straight ahead. She skied straight into it...

And then she was lying in the snow looking up at the sky. Right in the centre of it there was a perfectly round hole. As she watched, God leant out through the hole and pointed with his finger at the two men who had been following her.

She woke up, tense and shivering.

***

She'd have been even more worried if she'd known about a meeting between the salesman and the two men from the red car that same night.

"Why did you remove the girl?" the thin one demanded in a high, squeaky voice.

"It was obvious that you and your lapdog

there..." the salesman smiled sweetly at the gorilla, who scowled back, "were going the wrong way about it. No offence, but I'm afraid your approach was psychologically very unsound. She was much more likely to talk to someone non-threatening and intellectually stimulating like myself."

The thin man didn't smile. "And did she?" he asked coldly.

"Well, no. But she knows nothing. I tried her with the ozone layer and all the s's: both S.K.U.N.K. and Switzerland. None of them meant anything to her. It's the old man, her godfather, who has the knowledge to stop you, if anyone has."

This time, the thin man did smile. "Ah yes, the godfather. And he is not alone. This Hermann Souter is up to something. I think we will watch the godfather closely. What is it you English say? We will give him enough rope and he will hang not only himself, but all the others too."

5
The Hole in the Sky

isling hesitated as she reached the top of the hill. If S.K.U.N.K. or whoever were still watching the house, she'd better be careful. She left the road and made a detour to come out at the back of Seamus's house. Nobody appeared to be watching this side. She propped her bike up against the wall and scrambled over it into Seamus's back garden.

Somebody was up already: there was a light in the kitchen and, up in the attic, a glimmer of light escaped through the gap left by the jammed skylight blind. She wondered whether the wetness on the bushes was rain or just heavy dew; if it had rained in the night, Seamus must have got pretty wet. She grinned and knocked at the door.

Florence opened it, looking flustered. She frowned at Aisling. "I suppose you've come about your schoolbag. You were extremely lucky. Mrs Jackson found it last night when she was walking Toots. You'd think money grows on trees, the way you children treat your possessions. I left it in the hall. Go and get it quickly—I haven't time this morning for such shenanigans."

"Sorry." Aisling smiled meekly and went past her into the kitchen. It looked as if a bomb had hit it. The floor was covered with boxes of fruit and sacks of vegetables; the table overflowed with jars, tins, bottles and packets; and a heap of what looked like strips of dried meat lay on a plate on the sideboard. Beyond, in the hall, there rose a mountain of suitcases.

"Jeeps! How long are you going to be away for? Ten years?"

"Don't be impertinent, child." Florence rushed across the room to pull a pot back from the stove, just too late to stop it from boiling over. "I've had to go without once. I do not intend to do so again."

Aisling remembered how she had once made fun of Florence's obsession with food. Her mother had been very angry. She had told her that Florence had spent most of the last war in a Japanese prisoner-of-war camp in Malaya where she had lost both her husband and their baby son and had nearly died of starvation herself. It was no wonder, Mrs Daly had said, that she had a thing about food.

"Sorry," Aisling said again. "I'll just go up and see Seamus."

"I don't think you'd better. He's not in the mood for visitors."

"I won't stay."

Seamus's bed had been moved to the side of the studio and an old plastic bath had been placed under the broken skylight to catch the rain in the night. Aisling went straight to the bed. "You'll never guess what happened to me yesterday!"

"Out!" Seamus glared at her, then turned back to a box of paint brushes he was sorting through.

"Did you hear what I said?"

"Don't shout at me!" Seamus didn't look up. "Go away."

"S.K.U.N.K. tried to kidnap me!"

"Good."

Aisling leant over and removed the box. "S.K.U.N.K. tried to kidnap me yesterday when I left here," she repeated. "Don't you want to hear about it?"

"It doesn't look as if I have much choice."

"Honest!" Aisling took a deep breath and managed to control her temper. As calmly as she could, she explained what had happened the previous evening.

Seamus listened in silence. He frowned. "That's worse than I thought. We must be careful. If they get hold of any of the parts now, Hermann won't be able to assemble the machine. It will be the end of the world as we know it, my girl. That much is certain."

"What machine? Is it something that can mend holes in the ozone layer? I thought nobody could do anything except stop making them."

"It's the only chance we have. If all the parts are ready and we can get them to him safely, then maybe—just maybe—his machine can reverse what S.K.U.N.K. are doing."

"Please, Seamus. What's S.K.U.N.K.? And what are they supposed to be doing?"

"Did you ever hear the story about the elephant with the insatiable curiosity?" Seamus grumbled. "Still, I suppose it can't do any harm to tell you this much. Somehow, S.K.U.N.K. have managed to make a hole in the ozone layer in the stratosphere. Perhaps by sending up huge quantities of the chemicals which break up with light to release chlorine atoms. I don't know. It's blackmail on a huge scale. They have, I don't doubt, already warned various heads of government that, if they don't get what they want, they'll continue to keep this hole open."

"Can't anyone stop them?"

"No doubt people are trying. But, if we leave it to the powers that be, we might be too late. The hole itself will close up eventually, if left alone, but the longer it's there, the more damage it will cause. Hermann has designed a machine to counteract the effect of chlorofluorocarbons. We were hoping to try it out in the Arctic soon. But it looks, now, as if it will have to be given its trial run here in Europe. Which is why I am taking my own part of it to Switzerland. Which is why you are getting out of here and leaving me in peace."

"I don't get it," said Aisling. "If Hermann has made a machine, how do you have a part of it here?"

"Designed, I said. Not made. Other people are making various different parts for him."

"Other people? Who else, then?"

Seamus sighed. "If I tell you, will you promise to go away and leave me alone?"

"Cross my heart and hope to die," said Aisling.

"Hmpf," snorted Seamus. "All right then, but you won't understand. I shall tell you once and you may ask no questions and then you will go and I shall get on with my packing."

Aisling was tempted to say she thought Florence was doing that, but decided it was more sensible not to. She tried to look intelligent instead.

"There are six inventors, all friends of Hermann, in different parts of the world. One, as it happens, from each continent (except Antarctica, of course), though this is just a coincidence. I assume you do know what the continents are?"

Aisling ignored his sarcasm. "Africa, Asia, North and South America, Australasia and Europe," she said slowly. "You must be Europe."

"How did you guess?"

"But if Hermann lives in Switzerland, he must be Europe too."

"God grant me patience! If sheep eat grass and cows eat grass, does that make a sheep a cow? I told you Hermann designed the machine. He will assemble it, if all the parts are ready. That's why we have to bring him my part as soon as possible."

"And if this machine works, it'll sort out the

problem at the poles too?"

"If it works. It hasn't even been assembled yet, remember, let alone tested. But, if it works it'll at least keep things going until we can find S.K.U.N.K.'s headquarters and destroy them."

"Are you going to do that too?" Aisling tried to keep her voice serious. The idea of Seamus, a crotchety old invalid, and Florence, even with her crossbow, taking on an international gang of criminals was priceless.

Seamus glared at her. "I knew telling you was a waste of time. Get out."

Aisling put on her keen student look, the one which nearly always managed to fool Mr Duggan in maths class. "I'm sorry. Please! Just explain a bit more. I'm trying to understand."

Seamus didn't fall for it. "I have explained it to you. I've kept my side of the bargain, now you keep yours. Good bye."

"But—"

"Out!"

"Rats." Aisling slammed the door and thumped downstairs. If the world was in so much danger, surely Seamus would need all the help he could get. Yet he treated her like a child. It wasn't fair.

As she passed the door to the spare bedroom, she heard a plaintive miaowing sound. She opened the door and Mulligan streaked out. He bolted down the stairs like a one-cat herd of furry orange elephants. Whoever talked about the silence of a cat's footstep must have been joking, she thought, as she watched him skid round the corner at the foot of the stairs and disappear into the kitchen.

Florence didn't sound too pleased to have his company. In fact, Aisling realized, it was probably Florence who had shut him in the bedroom in the first place, to keep him out of the way. Just like they were trying to keep her out of the way. It would serve Florence right to have him under her feet again.

"Double rats," she said. She picked up her schoolbag, slung it over her shoulder and opened the front door.

She jumped.

There, standing on the step, his hand hovering over the bell, was a very tall, very thin young man wearing patched jeans, runners and a sweatshirt with *Health is Wealth* written across his chest.

"Morning!" he said with a friendly grin.

6
Dermot

ello," said Aisling warily. She started to close the door.

The young man stuck his foot in it. "Dermot," he said. "At your service. House-trained and really quite harmless. Seamus is expecting me."

Aisling looked at him suspiciously. "How do I know that?"

"Because I told you, isn't that right?"

Aisling pushed hard against the door. She couldn't close it.

"Now is that any way to greet the Fifth Cavalry, come to rescue you all? You should be throwing your arms around me with joy, isn't that right? I have arrived and Mafeking has been relieved."

"I don't know what you're talking about. Go

away or I'll call Seamus."

"What a good idea." The thin young man whistled into the grating by the door. "Dermot to Seamus! Dermot to Seamus! Are you receiving me?"

"Stop messing about." Seamus's voice was even testier than usual. "Will you get a move on and come up here. We haven't got all day."

"I know, I know and I couldn't agree with you more. But first you'll have to call off your faithful watchdog here, isn't that right?"

"Sorry." Aisling opened the door. "I thought you might have belonged to S.K.U.N.K. They were watching the house last night."

Dermot looked round. "Well, they don't seem to be doing so now. Are you coming to give me a hand?"

Aisling hesitated. She wondered what Seamus would say. And time was getting on . If she stayed much longer, she'd be late for school. Still, what the heck. She put down her bag again. "Okay."

As Dermot stepped through the door, an orange thunderbolt hurtled out of the kitchen, whammed into his legs, scrambled up them, clawed its way across *Health is Wealth* and arched itself round his neck.

"Morning, Mulligan." Dermot stroked the

purring cat.

"Jeeps! You don't have any raw liver in your pockets or anything, do you?"

Dermot grinned. He tickled Mulligan under the chin. "It's your own fault, isn't that right? If you will give the impression that all you live for is food, you can't expect people to appreciate your noble soul."

"Suffering catfish!" He stared at the sea of boxes, crates and bags as Moses might have stared at the Red Sea before it parted. "FLORENCE!"

Florence came scuttling from her kitchen. She dried her hands on her pinny, took off her glasses, wiped the steam from them and put them on again. Her face lit up. "Dermot!"

Dermot put his thin arms round her plump shoulders and hugged her tightly. Her feet dangled helplessly six inches from the floor. "And what do you think you're grinning at?" she asked Aisling as he put her down again. She patted her curls back into place. "Give Dermot a hand with these stores, child."

Dermot looked at the boxes again. "You're a great woman, Florrie. I've said it before and I'll say it again. You're one of the most well-organised women I know. Only..." He hesitated. "Don't you think that maybe we've

got a little too much stuff here, wouldn't you
say? We don't want to overload the truck now,
do we? Isn't that right?"

"Every item has been carefully considered,"
Florence said firmly. "I have had to go without
once: I don't intend to go without again. Every
eventuality must be covered. In an emergency,
we don't want to rely on others. We must be self-
sufficient."

"I know, I know. And you're so right. Only we
have to consider the facilities we have at hand,
isn't that right? If you think of the size of my
truck and then think of the size of Seamus's bed
and then think of the provisions you have
here... Do you see what I mean?"

Florence frowned. "All right," she said. "I'll
go through my list again and be absolutely
ruthless. But don't blame me if we run out of
something vital just when we need it most."

"Just you do what you can, Flo. That's the
best any of us can do. Isn't that right?"He
winked at Aisling. "Come on. Let's get the cases
on board and then we can start moving what
Florrie has left. Okay?"

Aisling picked up a case and followed him out
into the street. She looked for a truck—there
was no sign of one. The only vehicle parked near
the house was an exceedingly big oil-tanker

painted in bright orange-and-yellow stripes like a tiger, with huge, yard-high black letters on the side:

PARACETALOXYDIOCLORINITROGLYCERSULPHIDE
GAS
HIGHLY DANGEROUS!!!!!!
KEEP CLEAR!!!!!!

Underneath this was a skull and crossbones.

To Aisling's amazement, Dermot went straight to the tanker and started to fiddle with something at the back end. Aisling shrank back into the shelter of the doorway: *Promising young schoolgirl killed in mysterious explosion on Dalkey Hill...*

"Are you coming?"

She opened her eyes again. A door in the back of the tanker, which she hadn't noticed before because of the tiger stripes, had swung open and Dermot was waiting for her beside it. Somewhat warily, she went towards him.

"You jump in the back and I'll hand the cases up, okay?"

She looked at the skull and crossbones on the side of the tanker. "Okay," she agreed, she hoped nonchalantly.

Dermot gave her a leg up into the tanker. A

dark curtain hung inside the door, screening the interior. She pushed it aside. She gasped.

The inside of the tanker was like a room in a millionaire's mansion. Deep, soft, golden carpet covered the floor from wall to wall. Aisling heard her mother's voice: "Gold? And that deep a pile? However would I be able to keep it clean?" She grinned and walked across to a heater in the centre of the room. Around it were four deep, leather-covered armchairs. She sank into one. *Millionaire Aisling Daly arrives in New York...* She touched the chrysanthemums in a gleaming copper bowl on the small glass table in front of her; they were real.

"You going to fall asleep in there or are you going to give me a hand?"

She leapt out of the chair and went to help Dermot with the luggage. Even when Florence had stripped everything down to "absolute essentials," there seemed to be an awful lot. Dermot climbed in and helped her to stow everything away in an amazing number of cupboards concealed behind the oak panelling which lined the walls. He showed her the kitchen area behind a carved wooden screen on one side and a gold-and-brown bathroom on the other. "Neat, isn't it? Nothing but the best for Seamus, isn't that right?"

He pulled a lever beside him and a section of panelling swung down to reveal a bunk bed complete with gold-embroidered pillow and duvet. "There's two, but Seamus prefers his own bed, isn't that right? Which means I'd better go up and bring him down."

"Do you want any help?" Aisling wondered if she was strong enough. The way Dermot had been flinging suitcases and crates about had made her resolve to take fitness-training seriously in future.

"No need. It's only a question of fulcrums and the centre of gravity, isn't that right? I'll move the centre of gravity up to one end which should make lifting it no problem at all. Getting it round the bannisters and down the stairs might be a bit tricky, but we'll manage somehow, isn't that right?"

Aisling couldn't resist following Dermot up to the studio. Seamus was sitting up in bed with a tweed cape round his shoulders and a knitted balaclava helmet on his head. He glared at her. "I thought I told you to go. You'll be late for school."

"Can't I just—"

"Out!"

Muttering to herself, Aisling dawdled down the stairs. Above her she could hear Seamus giving orders: "A fraction to the left... No, up a bit... to the right... right, man! Now, round to the left again... watch that lampshade... Blast! Keep going... STOP!"

There was a crash.

Mulligan streaked down the stairs, his tail between his legs. Aisling looked up. Dermot must have tripped over the cat and practically dropped the bed. It was wedged up against the wall of the stairwell and Seamus had been thrown forward onto the duvet. His cape had flown over his head and the pillows had come to rest on top of him.

"There is nothing to laugh at, child." Florence was standing behind her. A quiver in her voice belied the criticism in her words and her eyes were twinkling behind her glasses. "You'd better go before he sees you again."

Aisling looked at the heaving mass in the bed above her. "You might be right. Bye! Have a good trip."

Florence gave her a kiss on the cheek and hurried upstairs to help with the bed.

Aisling slowly wandered out into the street.

7
The Tanker

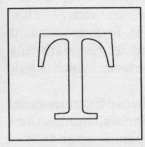

he door of the tanker was still open as she passed.

She was tempted to take a last look inside. After all, they'd be ages yet sorting the bed out and she was going to be so late for school that another few minutes wouldn't make any difference.

She sat down in the armchair again. It would be fantastic to travel to Switzerland, especially in a converted tanker like this. Thou shalt not covet, she thought with a grin. And anyway, did she really want to be chased by S.K.U.N.K. all the way to Switzerland? The thought of meeting the two men in the red car again—or the encyclopedia salesman—made her shiver. She got up.

On the way to the door, she noticed the lever Dermot had pulled earlier. She tried it and the bed fell forwards again. Just for fun, she slid under the duvet: *Lady Aisling Daly awaits her lover...* She turned over and snuggled the duvet around her.

She must have touched something: all of a sudden the bed started to move. Then everything went black. She forced herself to stay calm and felt around in the darkness, trying to find a catch or a lever which would bring the bed down again.

There was a crash. She heard Seamus swear and Dermot answer. Then more thumps came from the other side of the panelling as the bed was moved into position. The rear door of the tanker thudded to. Then the engine burst into life.

She was about to beat on the panelling to be let out, but stopped. Seamus's temper couldn't have been improved by the trip downstairs. He'd half-kill her if he knew she was here. Perhaps it would be better to wait until he'd calmed down a bit.

She listened to the noise of the engine. It was like being in a train with the blinds down or in a car with your eyes shut: she had the sensation of movement, smooth for the most part but more violent as Dermot swung the tanker round corners or braked at traffic lights but she had no idea how fast they were going or where they were.

The next thing she knew, the fat man who had followed her yesterday was trying to hold the pillow down over her head. She gasped for breath. He pressed the pillow tighter. She kicked and her foot hit the wooden panelling. She kicked harder, trying to get him off her, fighting for air.

There was a creak, a sharp jerk, and suddenly everything was bright again. The pillow and the fat man had gone. She sat up and gasped for breath.

Seamus's voice seemed to come from a long way away: "And just what do you think you're doing in there?"

She shook herself. "He was trying to smother me... He..."

Florence helped her out of the bed. "It's all right, child. You were having a nightmare. It's no wonder—you must have been half-suffocated. Come and sit down and I'll make you a nice cup of tea."

She settled Aisling in an armchair and went into the kitchen.

Seamus glared at her. "Well?"

"I was just trying the bunk and it shut up on me."

"No doubt Goldilocks had the same story."

"Honest. I only meant to look."

Seamus continued to glare. "And I suppose you think we'll turn round now and take you home? With a boat to catch? And maybe half of S.K.U.N.K. trying to see we don't make it?"

"Well, no... I mean, yes. I mean..."

Florence came back with a cup of sweet tea. She settled herself in the chair next to Aisling and picked up her knitting. "We can let her off in Rosslare. Nobody will worry about her till then; her mother will think she's at school and the school will think she's at home."

"That's right. Encourage her to play truant."

"I'm sure you played truant the odd time yourself, when you were at school. And it's only one day."

"Hmpf!" Seamus picked up a small pad which was lying on the duvet, turned his back on them and started to sketch.

Aisling supped the tea gratefully. When she had finished, she looked for something to do. Florence was knitting and Seamus sketching; neither looked as if they'd welcome bright conversation. She got up and selected a book from a shelf of books along one wall. She found she couldn't concentrate. She shut the book and stood up again.

Seamus threw down his pencil. "Will you stop jumping about like a guinea fowl on an ants' nest? If you're going to stay with us till Rosslare, find yourself an occupation."

"What?"

"I don't know. Paint a picture, write a novel, carve a log—just do something. And stop annoying me. I'm trying to think."

"She could keep an eye out behind to see if we're being followed," suggested Florence gently.

Aisling looked round. For the first time, she realized that there were no windows in the tanker. "How?" she asked.

Seamus groaned.

"Use the periscope, child," murmured Florence, worrying a needle into her knitting in search of a dropped stitch.

Aisling waited until she'd found it and restored it to its rightful place. "Where's the periscope?" she whispered.

Florence sighed and folded her knitting. "Up there." She pointed to a panel in the ceiling decorated with an Egyptian-looking painted eye.

Aisling considered the panel. It was at least three feet above her: even on tiptoe, it would be out of her reach. She looked for something to stand on. The coffee-table was too well-polished; she'd a feeling that Florence wouldn't like her to stand on that. The chairs, too, were probably a bad idea. She looked at Florence who had taken up her knitting once more, and at Seamus who was still busy sketching: she'd better not bother either of them again. She went into the kitchen area, pulled out a wooden chest labelled Finest Darjeeling Tea, carried it back to the main room and put it carefully under the panel with the eye. Both Florence and Seamus continued to ignore her completely.

Behind the panel she found a metal tube with fold-up handles. She pulled the tube and it slid easily down to a level with her face. Unfolding the handles, she looked into the viewfinder. Everything was black. She turned a knob at the base of the tube and the tube slid up into the daylight above the tanker.

It was fantastic! By using the handle to turn the tube, she could see all round the tanker: the road with fields stretching out on either side, houses, farms, low hills in the distance. She swept the horizon: *Aisling Daly sinks enemy warship!* she thought. *Torpedoes away!*

She must have spoken the last words aloud. "You're supposed to be keeping an eye on the road," Seamus growled. "Not playing games."

"Sorry." She turned the periscope until she had a clear view of the road behind. "There's a lot of traffic. It's difficult to know if something's following us or not."

"Hmm." Seamus picked up a walking stick which had been lying at the foot of the bed and pulled a speaking tube, just like the one in the studio, down from the ceiling towards him. "Slow down, Dermot," he ordered. "I want to check something."

"No problem." Dermot's voice came through a speaker in the wall. The tanker slowed suddenly.

"Well? Is there anyone still behind us?"

"Wait a minute," said Aisling. "They're only just starting to overtake now. There, that's most of them... Just a couple of lorries and one or two cars to go... Okay, that's the lot. Except..." her voice rose excitedly, "There's a red car that hasn't passed us. It's slowed down too. But it's too far behind to see who's in it."

"Use the zoom lens, you fool."

"Press the white button on the handle just above your left thumb," suggested Florence quietly.

Aisling did so. The car behind suddenly came so close that she was staring right through the windscreen. She jumped back quickly, falling off the tea-chest.

Seamus looked at her coldly. "What's the matter? Did something bite you?"

Aisling felt like an idiot. But it had shaken her to find herself what seemed like only inches away from the close-set, evil-looking eyes of the big fat man she'd been dreaming about only minutes ago. "It's them," she said. "The two men who tried to kidnap me yesterday."

"If you can manage to do so without falling off that thing again," Seamus growled, "I'd be obliged if you'd take another look and describe them to me. Properly."

She got back on the tea-chest and looked through the periscope again. Even though her reason told her that she couldn't be seen by the two men in the car, she still felt horribly exposed. The men, when she looked at them closely, seemed to be arguing with each other. She wondered what they were talking about: could it be the tanker? "You don't have a microphone attached to this thing too, do you?" she asked hopefully.

"No. Nor a soft drinks dispenser. I'm waiting for your description."

"The one that's driving," Aisling started off, "is big and fat with black hair cut the same length all round, sort of pudding-basin style.

He's got horrible piggy eyes and a big nose that looks as if it's been broken. He sort of looks as if he could have been a boxer. His mouth is all slobbery and he's got about five chins. He's disgusting."

"What's he wearing?"

"A scruffy black jacket and a black jumper with a high neck."

"And what about the other one?"

"Laurel? He's small and skinny and he's got short brown hair. He's wearing dark glasses so I can't see his eyes. The bottom half of his face sort of fades away. He's got a tiny nose and a very small mouth and hardly any chin. His face is sort of pear-shaped, really. He's wearing a jacket too—I think it's a suit, he's a lot smarter than Hardy, anyway—and a shirt and tie."

"Fine. Stow the periscope and come over here."

Aisling did so.

"Is that them?" Seamus showed Aisling the pad he'd been sketching on. To her amazement, the two men were drawn on it in almost perfect likenesses.

"That's them," she confirmed.

"Fine. Now, look in the bottom drawer there. You'll find a photograph album. Bring it here."

Seamus flicked over the pages. The whole

album was full of sketches of various men and women with names and dates written in underneath. He stopped at a sketch of two young men and put the sketch he had just made beside it. "What do you think?"

Aisling gasped. The two men in the album were obviously Laurel and Hardy, though they were at least twenty years younger.

She read the note underneath the sketch: Andrei Shavitov and Petrovich Lerntowski. S.K.U.N.K. Naples, June 16th, 1966.

Seamus scribbled the date at the bottom of the sketch he'd just made. "Stick that in the book, will you, child. The glue's in the top drawer, there. And then put it away. Dermot!" he shouted through the speaking tube. "Shavitov and Lerntowski are behind us in the red car. Lose them."

"Yes, sir! Hold on, everyone!" The tanker lurched forwards as he put his foot on the accelerator.

Aisling would have loved to have seen the chase which followed. Unfortunately, she was too busy holding on even to use the periscope. They were obviously travelling at a tremendous speed; then, suddenly, Dermot would brake and the tanker would slew violently round to the right or left; and then they'd go on again, racing until the walls vibrated.

It was just as well Dermot had taken the precaution of bolting Seamus's bed to the floor as the armchairs (including the one Florence sat in), the coffee table, the tea-chest and everything else which wasn't attached to the floor, walls or ceiling, slid backwards and forwards at every turn. Nothing moved very fast because of the deep pile of the carpet, but at one exceptionally bad jolt, the tea-chest bounced onto its side and slammed into a cupboard.

There was a loud miaow.

Aisling jumped.

Seamus had been sitting up in bed, his eyes shining with pleasure, as the tanker swayed back and forth. The smile left his face. "Who brought that orange monstrosity in here?"

Florence who had knitted placidly through all the jolting and jarring, continued to do so now.

Aisling went over to the cupboard, holding onto the wall to keep her balance. She opened the cupboard door: a frying pan, two saucepans and a metal sieve fell out. She crammed them back in, slammed the door shut, opened the door of the next cupboard and shut it again quickly when she saw the pile of glass and china inside.

"Come on, Mulligan," she whispered. "I know you're there."

There was no answer.

She raised her voice. "Puss, puss, puss! Here, Mulligan. Food for Mulligan!"

Immediately there was a miaowing and a scrabbling and a scratching from inside the tea-chest. She opened the lid. Mulligan jumped out and wove round her legs, purring like an overheated boiler.

"I asked who brought that shark-infested marmalade in here," repeated Seamus in ominous tones.

"I don't know," said Aisling. "I didn't."

"Well, you'd better feed him now he's here." Florence finally looked up. "There's cat food in the third cupboard from the end. Open the door carefully; I don't want it rolling about all over the place."

"Well, fancy that," observed Seamus drily. "Just by chance you happened to pack some cat food."

"You never know what may come in useful."

Aisling took a tin of WONDERKAT from the cupboard, opened it in the kitchen and spooned a generous measure into a saucer she found in the same cupboard. Mulligan fell on it as if he hadn't eaten for six months. There were two more plastic saucers: she debated putting milk and water into them but thought better of it— the tanker was still travelling far too fast. She waited until Mulligan had gulped down the food, then she looked for a floor cloth and wiped up the bits which had got onto the floor. It was obvious that nobody had ever told Mulligan when he was a kitten that cats are clean, fastidious animals.

Mulligan licked the last trace of WONDERKAT from his whiskers, rubbed up against Aisling as a thankyou and jumped onto Seamus's swaying bed where he flopped in an untidy heap. But for his almost inaudible purring, you would have thought he'd collapsed and died. Seamus moved his legs out of the way and regarded him thoughtfully.

"You realize we can't take him abroad with us," he said to no-one in particular. "There's a law about that sort of thing. And a sensible law it is, for once."

Nobody answered.

The tanker slowed down again and Dermot's voice came over the intercom. "Have a look for that red car again, Ash. I think we've shaken them off, isn't that right?"

Aisling looked. They were travelling along a

straightish bit of road through dull, grey-looking countryside. Using the telescopic lens, she scanned the road behind them. It was empty.

"Nothing," she reported. "They've gone."

"Fine." Seamus settled himself more comfortably. "It should be a clear run now to Rosslare."

8
Rosslare

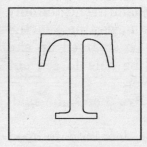hey arrived at Rosslare half an hour before the boat was due to sail. As Aisling got ready to leave the tanker Seamus, who had been dozing for the last hour or so, suddenly jerked awake. "Don't forget that blasted cat," he reminded her.

"I won't." She picked up the shopping basket in which Florence had settled Mulligan. It weighed a ton.

Florence handed her a huge packet of sandwiches and a bag of apples: "It's a long journey back to Dublin and we can't have you starving, child."

She was about to put them in the basket too when she thought better of it and stuffed them into her anorak pockets. Mulligan's nose twitched, but he stayed quiet.

She peered through the periscope. They were in the middle of a large car park. A grey removals van had stopped directly behind them but, by a stroke of luck, the driver had left the cab and it was empty. The cars on either side of the van did have people in them: in one, the only occupant was reading his newspaper; in the other, the windows were so steamed up she doubted if anyone would be able to see out anyway. It was now or never.

She went to the door. "Bye then," she said. "Good luck."

She opened the tanker door and jumped down.

To her surprise, Florence followed her. "I thought I'd buy a few bars of chocolate at the station," she said. "We might need them later."

Aisling thought of the tons of food already in the tanker and tried not to smile.

They slipped between the cars and lorries waiting for the boat. Aisling looked anxiously for the red car which had been following them: to her relief, there was no sign of it.

And then, just as they reached the station building, a man stepped out of the shadows.

Aisling grabbed Florence's arm. "Run!" she hissed.

Florence looked at her in surprise. "Really,

child. Whatever next?"

"Come, on!" Aisling tugged at her urgently.

The plump, middle-aged man stopped directly in front of them. He raised his hat to Florence. "Good afternoon, ma'am," he said cheerfully. "You must be Florence. Aisling's told me all about you. I'm delighted to make your acquaintance at last."

Aisling stared open-mouthed as Florence shook the encyclopedia salesman's hand. "I never..."

"Well, perhaps you didn't." The man beamed at her. He turned back to Florence. "And now you're off to France. You'll enjoy it. France, the centre of the civilised world: Paris! Brittany! Provence! It's a great pity Aisling wouldn't buy one of my encyclopedias—you could have read all about it."

Aisling tried again to drag Florence away. "Don't listen to him! Come on!"

"Don't blame Aisling, ma'am." The plumpish man gave another cheerful smile. "After all, we were never properly introduced. Smith's the name. John Smith. At your service, ladies."

Aisling fumed as Florence simpered at him.

He looked out to sea. "The weather doesn't look too great, I'm afraid. If it gets rough, you can't do better than CALM ANYONE pills. It just so happens that I have some with me here." He brought a small orange bottle out of his pocket. "Tested in three hundred and sixty four countries in conditions varying from a flat calm to a force ten gale and never failed to work. Only sixty pence a bottle. Would you like to try some?"

"No thank you," said Aisling quickly.

Florence smiled at him again. "I'm sure they are very good, er... Mr Smith. But I'm afraid I don't believe in drugs. Many thanks all the same. And now, if you'll excuse us, we have to go. It has been a pleasure meeting you."

"I'm sure we'll meet again soon. And don't forget, if the weather improves and you decide to go out on deck, make sure you wear plenty of suntan lotion. You can get badly burnt, even in a haze, quite apart from the risk of skin-cancer these days. It's dangerous times we live in. You ought to watch out." The man winked at Aisling, raised his hat to Florence again and turned away.

"He's a S. K. U. N. K. agent!" Aisling warned Florence as soon as he was out of earshot. "He was the third one at the house the other day."

"Oh. He seemed very nice to me. And didn't you say he had actually saved you from these two ruffians who were following us this morning?"

"Well... yes. But..."

"Exactly. Hurry up now, or you'll miss your train. And you have to phone your parents too, to let them know where you are and what time you'll be arriving. Your mother will be beginning to worry why you're not home yet."

At the station, Florence bought Aisling's ticket, checked the time of the Dublin train and left her at the phone box. Aisling's heart sank as she watched the tiny figure in the pink coat and rose-coloured hat scuttle across the platform to the kiosk.

Don't be a baby, she told herself. You've been on a train before. And S. K. U. N. K. won't be interested in you now. They'll be following the tanker, if they're anywhere at all. She opened the basket and tickled the top of Mulligan's head. *Aisling Daly, the famous zoologist, brings a fabulous orange creature back to Dublin.*

Mulligan yawned, stretched himself, and went back to sleep.

Aisling dialled 10 for the operator and asked for a reversed charges call to Dublin. While she waited for him to contact her mother and ask whether she'd pay for a call from Rosslare (she could just hear her mother's voice: "*Rosslare?*") she gazed idly out through the glass at the people passing by.

To her horror, a familiar figure came down the platform. It was the window cleaner! She shrank into the corner of the kiosk and turned her back. Her skin crawled as she waited for him to open the door.

The operator's voice caught her by surprise. "Go ahead, now, Rosslare. You're through."

She turned round carefully. The window cleaner had disappeared.

"Aisling! Whatever are you doing in Rosslare?"

"It's a long story." Aisling hesitated. She had to warn Seamus. She thought quickly, took a deep breath and decided. "I'm on my way to Switzerland with Seamus and Florence, Mum. I can't talk now, but I'll be okay. Everything's fine. I'm afraid I don't know when we'll be back, but I'll send you a postcard. I have to rush now, the boat's just leaving. Bye!"

"Aisling! Wait a minute! You can't—"

Aisling put the receiver down firmly. Well, she thought, that was that. Now to get back to the tanker.

She picked up the basket again before her courage failed her and humped it out of the station back to the car park. Fortunately there was no sign of the window cleaner.

She stopped, horrified. The car park was deserted. She could just see the last car in the distance, disappearing up the ramp into the hold of the ship. What on earth was she going to do now? She watched as the ramp was raised. There was no way she'd be able to get on board without a ticket and she didn't even have a passport with her. In a way it was a relief; at least there was no more she could do.

Picking up the basket again, she trudged back to the station.

9
Stowaway

he train from Dublin had just come in and the station was now full of people. A party of schoolchildren came down the platform, shepherded by a tall scrawny teacher whose shoulder-length hair flopped over his eyes and whose scarf trailed from his neck onto the platform behind him.

"Hurry up, you lot! We'll miss the boat. Edward! Get back into line! How am I supposed to know how many of you we've lost if you keep milling about like that? Stand still, blast you!"

He walked down the line, counting the pupils. They kept moving and he had to keep starting again. Aisling watched, amused.

And then she realized how she could get on the boat!

She waited until the teacher had gone back to

the front of the line and approached the nearest group of pupils. "I've got to get to France," she said urgently. "I've..." What reason could she give? "I've run away from home! My stepfather's following me. He'll kill me if he catches me. I've just got to get to France and find my real Dad. Can you lot help me?"

"Ace!" said a tall girl with blond hair. "How?"

"If I'm in the middle of your group, I might be able to get onto the boat without being seen. There's so many of you, maybe no-one will notice there's one extra."

"Sure, O'Driscoll wouldn't notice if there were twenty extra." A red-haired boy with a Cork accent grinned at her. "It's worth a try."

"I don't know...:" One of the girls looked anxious. "I think we should tell. We could get into trouble."

"Come on, Helen. Don't be so wet." The others looked at her in disgust.

"What's your name?" asked a small boy with glasses.

"Aisling."

"Okay, Aisling. We'll give it a try."

It worked.

***

She left the group as soon as they were on board the boat. She wanted to get to the tanker as quickly as possible, before she was seen by the window cleaner or anyone else from S.K.U.N.K. At the moment, there were too many people around. She slipped into the ladies' washroom to wait until things had quietened down. At least neither Shavitov, Lerntowski, nor the window cleaner (nor the mysterious John Smith) could find her there.

The boat shuddered as the engines started. Then the floor of the washroom began to heave gently up and down: they were moving. She glanced down at her feet; the basket was moving too. Mulligan, who had stayed admirably quiet for an amazing amount of time, had woken up and was obviously feeling hungry.

Quickly, before any of the ladies in the washroom could see what was happening (she was sure it was illegal to bring a cat aboard a ship), she took a sandwich out of the packet Florence had prepared and stuffed it into the basket. The basket shook as Mulligan devoured it. She gave him another to keep him going, picked up the basket and left the washroom.

She followed the signs past the cabins to the car deck. Fortunately not many people were about—presumably they were all watching the ship leave port—and she saw no-one she recognized.

As she descended the ladder and was pushing back the sliding door which led to the car deck, a ship's officer came through towards her. "Sorry miss. No-one's allowed down here now. Not until the boat docks again."

"But I left something in the car."

"Then you'll have to do without. Now, back to your Mammy with you."

The officer waited for her to go up the ladder ahead of him. Aisling cursed silently. Now what was she going to do? She could hardly hide in the washroom until they reached France. She had to get to the tanker.

She pretended to look at a slot machine at the top of the stairs while the officer went past her. He disappeared into the lounge and she sneaked back down the companionway.

Would he have locked the door?

To her relief, it slid open when she tried it. She stepped into a huge reverberating cavern lit by harsh fluorescent light. The cars and lorries were arranged in rows, packed as tightly as sardines. She edged her way along the metal wall, searching for the tanker. At least she couldn't mistake it, she thought with a grin, as she made out its brightly-striped shape ahead of her.

She edged her way between the parked cars until she'd reached it. The cab was empty. For a moment her heart sank, and then she realized that Dermot would have had to leave his vehicle like all the other drivers.

She went round to the back of the tanker and tapped on the door. "It's me," she whispered. "Aisling!"

Nothing happened for a minute, and then a flicker in one of the blobs forming the zigzag across the tanker's rear indicated that someone was using the peephole in the door. Florence opened the door. She didn't say anything as Aisling climbed in.

There was an appetising smell in the tanker which made Aisling's mouth water. Mulligan leapt out of the basket like a rat from a trap and skidded round the screen into the kitchen. Florence shut the tanker door and followed him, leaving Aisling to face Seamus alone.

He glared at her. "I take it you have an excuse for this?"

"I thought…"

"I doubt if you did. I made it abundantly clear to you that you had no business sneaking aboard this tanker in Dublin. And now you have the gall to follow me here. Do you realize, child, that this is a dangerous mission? How can I do what I have to do if I have to play nursemaid to you all the time?"

Aisling had never heard him so angry.

"I'm sorry," she said meekly. "I only wanted to warn you. I saw the window-cleaner at the station. I'm sure he was following you too."

"Hmm." Seamus looked thoughtful. "It was too much to hope, I suppose, that we'd shaken them off. I wonder if they'll try anything on the boat?" He smiled. "I don't fancy their chances if they do."

The prospect of danger seemed to restore his good humour. "Well then, now you're here, you might as well make yourself useful. Go and help Florence with the supper."

10
The Car Ferry

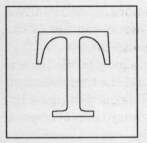he meal was as good as it smelt. Aisling's family had a mobile home at Brittas and she was used to convenience foods on holidays—hamburgers, beans, easy one-pot dishes. Florence believed in eating properly and Aisling, as she tucked into soup, followed by steak, baked potatoes and fresh vegetables, was extremely grateful. Afterwards, she washed the dishes in the tiny kitchen, helped Florence to tidy the main "room," read for a little and then went to bed, taking care this time not to touch the lever which closed the bunk.

She woke in the early hours of the morning. Seamus was snoring gently in his huge brass bed and Florence was fast asleep too, in the bunk opposite. Aisling went to the kitchen to make herself a drink. Mulligan, who had been sprawled across the foot of Seamus's bed, apparently equally sound asleep, reached the fridge before her. With a sigh, she poured him a saucer of milk. She looked at her watch: nearly 5 a.m. And they wouldn't be in Le Havre until after lunchtime. It was so boring, stuck in the tanker. And stuffy, too, down in the hold. She could do with a breath of fresh air.

The more she thought about it, the more claustrophobic she felt. Could she risk going out into the ship again? Everyone would be asleep, and all she wanted was a couple of minutes on deck, just to look at the sea and get some air. After all, she told herself, it was probably the only chance she'd ever have of seeing what it was like to be on a ship—her family never had the money for trips abroad, like her friend Louise's did.

Quietly, she raised the periscope and scanned the deck. It was deserted. She tiptoed to the back of the tanker, slipped through the curtain and noiselessly pulled the lever which operated the door.

As she had hoped, the corridors were deserted and the few people who didn't have cabins and who were huddled in blankets on the reclining seats in the lounge, all seemed fast asleep when she crept past the door. She stepped out onto the upper deck.

The night air hit her like a blast from a freezer. She shivered. Thank goodness she'd thought of bringing her anorak. She looked over the rail. The sea was rolling in great mountains whose sheer sides fell away into awesome black caverns. The moon, tossed about by wild black clouds, spread an eerie silver light across the crests of the huge waves. The ship shuddered as it ploughed through the heaving sea (John Smith had been right about the weather) but, despite not having taken any of the CALM ANYONE pills, Aisling didn't feel in the least bit sick.

She pulled up the hood of her anorak: *Aisling Daly leads her convoy through the Arctic wastes...* She scanned the horizon with cold, calculating eyes, watching for ice floes or a sign of the enemy fleet.

After about ten minutes, her hands were blue. She decided it was time to go back down to the tanker. At the top of the second flight of stairs, a space-invaders machine caught her eye. She felt in her pocket, found a fifty pence piece and put it in the machine. Enemy spaceships swarmed across the screen. Grasping the control handle firmly, she started to fight back: *Space captain Daly decimates*

Martian hordes...

"Not bad at all," said a voice at her elbow as she wiped out her third enemy ship. "Mind you, if you'd studied Volume 11 of the *Encyclopedia for the Expansion of Young Minds* under V for Velocity, you'd have realized that the drag coefficient minus velocity added to your reaction time on the trigger would... Ah, but now you've let the rest get away. I hope I didn't distract you."

Aisling stared at him open-mouthed.

"What am I doing here?" asked the salesman cheerily. "Travelling abroad, same as you. My mission is not only to expand young minds on our native islands. I have here," he patted the briefcase under his arm, "a sample of both the French and the German translations of our excellent encyclopedia. Why should our offer stop at the Channel, I ask you? Does not the Continent, too, need enlightening?"

"Excuse me." Aisling tried to speak as calmly as possible. "I have to go."

To her surprise, the salesman made no attempt to stop her. "An excellent idea. It wouldn't help Seamus, after all, if you were caught as a stowaway."

Aisling looked at him sharply. "I don't know what you're talking about," she said stiffly.

"Goodbye."

"Au revoir." The salesman smiled. "See Volume 3 under F for French. It means until we see each other again. Which I'm sure won't be long."

Aisling went downstairs thoughtfully. Who on earth was John Smith? And how did he know so much about her? If he was a S.K.U.N.K. agent, why was he making himself so obvious? And why had he saved her from Shavitov and Lerntowski in Dalkey? She just couldn't work it out.

As she passed the sign saying Cabins again, her way was blocked by a little old lady struggling with a heavy suitcase. Aisling stood aside to let her pass.

"I vonder if you could help me viz my luggage?" The little old lady's eyes glinted behind her rimless glasses and a hairpin, escaping from her bun, fell to the floor.

"Of course," said Aisling automatically. She put out a hand to take the case.

"No, not zat one. I can manage zat. Zere is anozer one in my cabin—number six." She waited for Aisling to fetch it.

Aisling squeezed past her and went into the cabin. A brown leather suitcase was lying on the floor beside the bunks. She picked it up. Behind her the door slammed shut.

She turned, put the case down, and tried the handle. It didn't budge. I can't have locked myself in, can I? she thought. She banged on the door. "Sorry," she shouted. "I can't open the door. Can you try it from that side?"

There was no answer. The little old lady had had a foreign accent; perhaps she didn't understand. Aisling sat down on the bottom bunk. *Promising young schoolgirl found starved to death in second class cabin,* she thought. Unlikely, though. They'd find her when they cleaned the ship, which they'd have to do in Le Havre. Only Dermot and the tanker would have gone by then and she hadn't a ticket. Or a passport. She had to get back to the tanker before anyone found her.

She banged on the door again. She felt stupid shouting "Let me out! Let me out!" but it seemed the only thing to do, so she did it.

Almost immediately she saw the door handle turning. Of course, the little old lady wouldn't go off and leave her; she'd want her suitcase back. Relieved, she stepped back to let the door open.

The window cleaner came into the cabin. He shut the door behind him and smiled nastily. "Sure, it's a fine little Child of Mary you are!"

His voice sent shivers down her spine. "That'll learn you to help old ladies."

Aisling backed against the wall, keeping the suitcase between herself and the man. Why hadn't she been more suspicious? If she'd only thought, she'd have realized it was most unlikely that anyone would be leaving their cabin in the middle of the night. *Super sleuth Aisling Daly outwits the baddies!* What a laugh.

She looked desperately round for a communication cord, like they have on trains, or anything else that would help her, but there was nothing.

The man threw the suitcase on the bunk and grabbed her. He twisted her arm behind her back. She gritted her teeth.

"Okay, then. Where's Seamus's bleeding machine?"

"I don't know what you're talking about."

"Oh yes you do. I'm talking about the machine S.K.U.N.K. wants and I'm talking about the two ould wans in the tanker. And don't you go thinking we won't get into the tanker. We won't even need to break into it now that we've got you to bargain with. Your grandaddy will open to us before you can say Pat Flaherty, so he will."

"He's not my grandfather." Aisling tried to

sound confident. "So don't expect him to care. And he's got guns and secret weapons and things. You'll never get in."

The window cleaner gave an evil smile. "You want to bet? Now is that bleeding machine on the boat or isn't it?"

"I told you I don't know about any machine. What would Seamus have a machine for anyway? He's an artist."

"Sure, you wouldn't be trying to be funny now, would you kid? I'm a nice friendly fella, but if you start giving me lip…" He twisted Aisling's arm so that she gasped with pain. "Now be a good girl and tell Uncle Pat just where it is or I'll have to hand you over to them Russkies. And they are not nice fellas, sure they aren't."

Aisling didn't say anything.

The window cleaner looked disappointed. "All right, then. Don't say I didn't warn you. Come on. I suppose I'd better take you to the boss. But don't try anything on the way or I'll break your bleeding arm, see." He twisted Aisling's arm again so that a sharp pain shot through her shoulder. "Sure, wasn't it lucky for me I saw you on deck there? The boss'll be delighted. You never know when a hostage will come in useful, sure you don't."

He opened the door carefully. The sweet little

old lady was standing just outside it with her suitcase: her twinkling black eyes were as hard as ice as she watched him drag Aisling out of the cabin. "Zank you most kindly, young lady," she said sweetly. "Vat a pity you cannot help me viz my cases after all. Take her down to ze ozer cabin, Pat. Zey vill be zere soon. And see zat she does not get avay."

"She won't." The window cleaner shifted his grip to Aisling's wrist and dragged her towards the staircase. A young couple was coming up the stairs towards them. Aisling tried to pull her hand away. "Help!" she yelled. "I'm being kidnapped!"

"That's enough, now, Mary!" The window cleaner spoke sharply. "Will you ever stop making a show of me?"

Aisling grabbed the woman with her free hand. "Please help me! Fetch the police or something!"

"She's a dreadful child for playing games, Missus. Sure, doesn't she take after her Mam, God rest her, in imagination. Here, Mary—just you stop annoying the people and come along with me like a good girl. She watches too much telly, so she does," he explained to the young man. "Come on, now, Mary. Get a move on." And he dragged Aisling, still protesting, down the stairs.

The couple parted to let them through. "Kids," Aisling heard the man say. "Better him than me. Who'd want to be a father?"

It was useless. There was only one thing left to try.

Near the foot of the stairs, she pretended to trip. The man grabbed the rail with one hand and jerked her back with the other, so hard she thought her arm had come out of its socket.

"What's the bleeding game, then?" he asked suspiciously. "You stop messing about or I'll break every bone in your body, so I will."

Aisling was crouched on the floor as if in agony. "Ouch!" she moaned. "I've done something to my leg. I think I've broken it."

"Stand up!"

"I can't."

The man let go of Aisling's hand and bent down to lift her up forcibly. She uncoiled like a jack-in-the-box, butted him in the stomach and sent him reeling backwards. He fell, winded, over a corner of the stairs. His head crashed against the steel wall.

Before he could recover, Aisling rushed down the next flight of stairs, through the doorway to the car deck and dodged through the line of cars to the tanker. She banged on the back door. "Let me in! It's me! Aisling! Hurry up! I'm being followed!"

There was a flicker of movement at the peephole again and the door opened. Florence helped her in.

Seamus was sitting up in bed. "Well?" he asked irritably. "Now what?"

"I haven't time to explain," panted Aisling. "The window cleaner's after me."

There was a tremendous hammering at the door. "Open up!" roared a voice.

"That's him," hissed Aisling.

"Sit quiet." Seamus stayed infuriatingly calm. "It would take dynamite to break in here once the security system is on."

Sure enough, the hammering stopped.

"What's he doing?" whispered Aisling.

"Probably having a look round. Either that or frying eggs. What do *you* think he's doing?"

"He could wreck the engine."

"Huh."

Aisling looked to see if Florence was taking the matter any more seriously. She was quietly knitting in her armchair again, as if nothing were happening. But Aisling was relieved to see that she had taken her crossbow out and had put it, together with a quiver of bolts, on the coffee table beside her.

"Aren't either of you going to do anything?"

She was answered by the scream of a siren."

"What on earth is that? Have we struck a rock?"

Seamus grinned. "Our window cleaner seems to have touched the engine. I'd say that'll make him leave pretty quickly—assuming he's survived the electric shock. Have a look through the periscope and tell me what you see."

Aisling raised the periscope quickly. People were running from all directions to see what the commotion was about and the window cleaner, looking very ill, was just staggering away between two parked cars. "He's left," she reported. "And thousands of people are coming over to see what's up."

"I'd better stop the alarm then." Seamus pressed a switch above his head and the noise stopped. Aisling, watching through the periscope, saw the people gradually disperse.

"Do you think he'll try again?"

"Not at the moment. There's too many people about now and he won't risk making a fuss again. But we'll have to be careful when we get off the ship. Now, is there any chance of getting a bit of peace around here, or is that asking too much?"

Florence stood up and put away her crossbow. "What we need is a nice cup of tea."

"Huh," said Seamus. "That's your answer to everything, woman: a nice cup of tea."

"It helps," said Florence calmly. And she went into the kitchen.

***

As Seamus had predicted, S.K.U.N.K. left them alone and the rest of the morning passed peacefully, though painfully slowly.

Just after lunch, the noise of the engine changed: they were nearing France. Aisling longed to be on deck, watching the French coast coming nearer and nearer, seeing French houses and French countryside and French people for the first time in her life. But she didn't dare leave the tanker again.

Seamus had spent the morning reading the volume of the encyclopedia Aisling had brought with her to the house in Dalkey and drawing in his sketchbook. He now began to look at his watch and drum his fingers impatiently on his duvet.

"Where's that health freak? He can't still be jogging round the deck. He should have been back by now."

Florence dealt with a particularly difficult part of her knitting before replying. "He'll come."

"Huh." Seamus frowned at her. "It was your idea to use him as a driver. Just remember that."

"He'll be fine. He made a mistake last time and he's paid for it. He won't do the same again."

"I wish I was as sure as yourself. Despite all his muscles, he's a weakling, is your Dermot. And I doubt if prison's made that much difference to him."

"Was Dermot in prison?" Aisling was horrified. "Why's he driving us, then?"

"Because Florence likes lame dogs," grunted Seamus.

"I'm surprised at you, Aisling," Florence chided. "Just because someone's been in prison once, doesn't mean they cannot reform themselves. Dermot has reformed and it is only fair to give him another chance. Mulligan adores him," she added. "And Mulligan is a great judge of character."

Seamus raised his eyes to the roof of the tanker. "Now I've heard everything!" he said in disgust.

Aisling looked through the periscope again, to see what was happening outside. The car deck was busy with people returning to their vehicles. Some of the drivers had already started their engines. But there was no sign of Dermot or, thank goodness, of any of the S.K.U.N.K. agents either. What would happen if Dermot didn't turn up? *Irish stowaways found in abandoned chemical tanker...*

"Maybe S.K.U.N.K.'s caught him," she said. "No... Wait a minute!" Someone came through the door from the upper deck. "Here he is now!"

She felt the colour leave her face. "Seamus!" she whispered urgently. "There's something wrong with him. He can hardly walk. And..." she gulped, "the man who's helping him is John Smith or whatever his name is—the encyclopedia salesman!

11
France

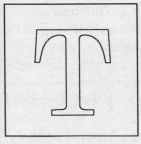hey heard the crash of the cab door slamming and then a voice Aisling was beginning to know all too well came over the intercom.

"Evening all!" said the encyclopedia salesman cheerfully. "Are you receiving me?"

"Loud and clear," Seamus replied coldly. "I gather I have the pleasure of addressing John Smith?"

"None other. You must be Grandad. I'm delighted to meet you at last."

"If you have mislaid your grandfather, I suggest you look elsewhere," Seamus said, even more coldly. "I am not he. And I should like to speak to my driver."

"Sorry, Grandad." The encyclopedia salesman sounded even more cheerful. "I'd love to let you speak to him. But, if you want my advice, I don't think you should bother."

"I don't want your advice." The pencil in Seamus's hand snapped in two. "And kindly allow me to be the judge of what's worth the bother or not. Let me speak to Dermot!"

"Certainly, Grandad. I was only trying to be helpful. If you insist, here he is."

There was a pause.

"Well?" snapped Seamus.

"Come on, Dermot. Speak up, lad. Grandad wants to hear from you."

There was another pause. Then, suddenly, Dermot's voice came through the microphone in an ear-splitting bellow. "Oh my beloved Seamus!" he sang. "I love him, yes, I love him!" He sounded like a berserk Italian ice-cream vendor. "And dear old Florence! She's a great woman, is Florrie, isn't that right? Three cheers for Flo! Hip, hip, hip..."

Aisling thought Seamus was about to have a heart attack. "That's quite enough!" he roared. "Pull yourself together, man. Are you drunk?"

"Me? Drunk?" Dermot's voice rose in indignation. "Never touch the stuff. It's bad for your health, isn't that right? Never, never touch..."

"You! Smith or whatever your name is!

What's going on?"

"Ah well," answered the salesman. "There you have me. I found him coming out of the second-class lounge singing

In Dublin's fair city
Where the girls are so pretty
I first set my eyes on sweet Florence O'Toole.
If I'd had time, I'd have checked under Volume 3: F for Folksongs. I could have sworn the original had something to do with a Molly Malone, but then, I may be wrong. It was very touching, whatever its authenticity. Obviously straight from the heart."

Aisling glanced at Florence. She continued to knit placidly. If she was aware of the conversation, she certainly gave no sign.

"Go on!" ordered Seamus.

"Well, he was just about to fall down the companionway, which wouldn't have been that good for his health (see Volume 8 under P for Physical Fitness, Aisling), so I gave him a hand and brought him here."

"And I suppose you expect me to be grateful?"

"No need, Grandad. I've been wanting to get to know you for a long time. I take it you're not interested in buying an encyclopedia?"

"Not at the moment."

"Pity."

Seamus flicked through his sketch pad until he found the sketch he'd made from Florence's description of the salesman at Rosslare. He examined it thoughtfully. Then: "Can Dermot drive?"

"I wouldn't say so, Grandad. We've only got another few minutes before we dock and he won't have recovered by then. That stuff takes at least a couple of hours to wear off."

"What stuff?" Aisling asked quickly.

"Sorry?"

"She asked what stuff."

"The stuff they put in his drink, of course," said the salesman. "See Volume 7 under M for Mickey Finn."

"Never," said Dermot thickly, "Nobody's never slipped me a Mickey... Mickey... Whatsits. Isn't that right? Course I can drive. Never felt better." The horn suddenly blared and Dermot started roaring "Brrrrrrr, peep-peep, brrrrrrr..." at the top of his voice.

"Stop that!"

"Yes, Seamus. Of course, Seamus."

"You are obviously in no fit state to drive." Seamus spoke more to himself than to anyone else. "So what do we do now?"

"I know. Florrie will drive! Good old Florence! Flo can do anything, isn't that right?"

"Florence doesn't exist," the salesman told him patiently. "Not in the eyes of the customs officials, anyway. It looks as if I'll have to drive you all myself. It's just as well my licence is in order."

"But..." Aisling looked at Seamus in horror.

He switched off the intercom. "But what, child? He's right. Dermot can't drive and the rest of us officially don't exist. So, unless you've a better idea, we'll just have to risk it."

"I trust him." Florence spoke quietly.

"You would," said Seamus. "No doubt that damned cat likes him too."

"Mulligan hasn't met him yet, but it wouldn't surprise me if he did. He's a wise cat. However, I am not trying to influence you one way or the other, I am just stating a fact. I trust him. And you know I'm usually right in these matters."

"Hmm." Seamus thought for a minute. Then he switched on the intercom again. "All right," he said. "I'll leave you to get us through customs. You'll find the papers in the glove compartment. Everything should be in order. Over and out."

A few minutes later the ship's engines changed pitch, there was a great shuddering and jolting, the ship gave a final heave, and then there was silence.

They had arrived in France.

***

They disembarked without incident: the customs delayed them for about half an hour while they checked Dermot's documents and looked at John Smith's licence. It appeared, from the fact that he was allowed to continue driving, to be not only in order, but also to qualify him to drive a tanker of dangerous chemicals across Europe, a fact which Aisling, anyway, found highly suspicious.

S.K.U.N.K. was certainly well organised, she thought. And, despite Florence's intuition, Aisling believed more and more strongly that John Smith belonged to S.K.U.N.K.

She kept a watch at the periscope, expecting an ambush at any minute, but nothing happened. John Smith drove the tanker straight through Le Havre and out along the main road east towards Switzerland. Aisling wasn't reassured. The others might trust him, but at least she would keep up her vigil. He could turn off anywhere and, unless she was looking through the periscope, they'd never know.

For the first hour or so, they were part of a

stream of cars and lorries which had come off the boat with them. Gradually, these either overtook them or fell behind until at last they were practically alone on the long grey road, apart from a small car in the far distance. It looked typically French but was making no effort to gain on them. Unfortunately, even with the telescopic lens, it was too far away to see who was in it.

"Could what's their names—Shavitov and Whatsits—have got another car?" Aisling asked.

"Lerntowski. It's possible, child. Quite possible. Why? Do you think they're following us again?"

"I'm not sure. But there's been a car behind us for some time."

"Keep an eye on it, then. There's no point in messing around here. We have to hurry. If it is them, we'll lose them later."

When Dermot's driving again, thought Aisling. So Seamus doesn't trust John Smith either!

On and on they travelled along the flat, poplar-lined road which traversed northern France. The day was grey and cold and the sky merged into the horizon in a band of dull grey mist. Aisling watched the long, straight road, the undulating fields, the tidy symmetrical poplar trees... She went over the route in her mind: Le Havre, Rouen, avoid Paris and north to Rheims, then south-east to Châlons-sur-Marne, Belfort, Basel. It was going to be a long drive.

As the afternoon wore on, she got sleepier and sleepier. She had to make an effort to stay at the periscope.

"Why don't you come down for a while?" asked Florence. "I'll wake you for supper."

"I have to watch the road." Aisling rubbed her eyes. They kept closing, no matter how hard she tried to concentrate.

"Nonsense," said Florence. "Mr Smith is obviously a safe driver. If I were your mother, I certainly wouldn't allow you to gad about as you were doing last night. A girl of your age needs her sleep. Pull your bunk out and go and lie down for a while."

"It's all right. I'm fine."

Aisling supported her head on her arm. It had become very heavy all of a sudden.

The next thing she knew, the tanker had stopped. She sat up with a jerk. "What's happened?"

Florence was still calmly knitting. Seamus was sitting up in bed with a tray in front of him.

The whole tanker smelt deliciously of roast beef and gravy and roast potatoes.

"Your food's in the oven." Florence looked up and smiled.

Aisling realized she was famished. She fetched her plate from the kitchen where Mulligan was hard at work licking a saucer clean of the last tiny scrap of food. He followed her out and sat in front of her on the carpet, balancing on his huge hindquarters with his front paws in the air and a pleading expression in his large yellow eyes. Aisling ignored him: Florence's cooking was too good to share with a cat. If doing without during the war led to meals like this, she thought, it's a pity her Mum hadn't been born twenty years earlier.

She wiped her mouth with the napkin Florence had provided. "That was fantastic!" And then she realized that she hadn't given a thought to S.K.U.N.K. or their position since she woke up. "Where are we?" she asked urgently. "How's Dermot? Who's driving us? Did the car behind catch up?"

"We are," Seamus informed her, "in Châlons-sur-Marne, a town the population, altitude and mean average rainfall of which our friend Smith would no doubt have at his fingertips. Dermot has, like yourself, slept most of the day.

We passed through Rheims an hour or so ago and saw no sign of a jackdaw. Does that answer your questions?"

"Jackdaw?" repeated Aisling. "Is that code for a S.K.U.N.K. agent?"

Seamus raised his eyes heavenwards. "Is there no end," he asked the ceiling, "to the ignorance of this generation? *The Ingoldsby Legends*, child. Have you never heard of 'The Jackdaw of Rheims'?"

"No," said Aisling. She was sure she was going to, however.

"*The Jackdaw sat on the Cardinal's chair,*" quoted Seamus. "*Bishop and abbot and prior were there.* And, if you hadn't been sleeping, you'd have seen the cathedral. Marvellous building. Joan of Arc crowned the Dauphin there in 1429."

Aisling felt that it was bad enough John Smith bombarding her with unwanted facts all the time, without Seamus starting too. "What's that got to do with S.K.U.N.K.?" she asked impatiently.

"Now, there's a thought." Seamus chuckled. "We could try the Cardinal's Curse on them. That ought to put them off, if nothing else does:

In holy anger, and pious grief,
He solemnly cursed that rascally thief!

He cursed him at board, he cursed him in bed;
From the sole of his foot to the crown of his
head;
He cursed him in sleeping, that every night
He should dream of the devil, and wake in a
fright;
He cursed him in eating, he cursed him in
drinking—"
"*He cursed him in coughing, in sneezing, in*
winking—"
added Florence.

Seamus took over again, rolling the words sonorously around the inside of the tanker:

"*He cursed him in sitting, in standing, in*
lying;
He cursed him in walking, in riding, in
flying,
He cursed him in living..." His voice fell dramatically, "*he cursed him in dying!*"

"Unfortunately, I fear it would affect our friends about as much as it did the pious congregation. Nobody seemed one penny the worse."

"Except the jackdaw," objected Florence.

"Let's hope that's an omen."

Aisling looked from one to the other in exasperation. "If you've quite finished," she said. "Why are we stopping here?"

"Why not?" asked Seamus. "It's as good a town as any."

If it had been possible to storm out and slam the door, Aisling would have done so.

Florence took pity on her. "Mr Smith and Dermot are eating," she said. "When they've finished, we'll go on again."

"Is that salesman coming with us all the way? Surely, if Dermot's all right now, we can get rid of him?"

"After all the help he's given us? That would be most ungrateful, child. Where would we be without him?"

Aisling appealed to Seamus. "You don't trust him either, do you?"

"Not especially. However, I don't imagine it can do much harm to let him tag along a bit further. Why don't you see if you can see them? They should be about finished eating by now."

Aisling looked through the periscope again.

It was dark outside. They were in a town square, facing a large flood-lit building on top of which flew a red, white and blue flag. If she remembered her French lessons with Madame Colombe correctly, it must be the *mairie* or town hall. She turned the periscope so that she could see more of the square: the tall thin houses had long narrow windows with faded shutters;

stubby, leafless trees, each guarded by an iron corset, edged the pavement; light spilled out of the Café des Amis directly opposite.

"There's no sign of them. Your man can't have kidnapped Dermot, can he?"

"Don't be silly, child."

"Out of the mouth of babes and infants..." Seamus quoted. "I don't trust that walking encyclopedia either. I'd feel safer if my accelerator weren't here."

"Your what?"

"The machine we're bringing to Hermann."

"You're as bad as Aisling," Florence said firmly. "Mr Smith is honest. I'm sure of it."

"All the same, I think we'll put Plan B into operation. Florence!"

Florence frowned at him. "It's quite unnecessary, I tell you."

Seamus acted as if she hadn't spoken. "Pack a bag for Aisling here. And give me the belt you'll find in that bottom drawer."

Florence sighed and took a leather belt with a pouch in it out of a drawer at the foot of the bed. Seamus removed the box from beneath his pillow. He unlocked it, checked the machine, and locked the box carefully again. It just fitted into the pouch on the belt.

"Here. Tie this round you. And guard it with

your life, do you hear? Keep the key separate."

"Er... yes." *Schoolgirl dies fighting off international gang of criminals!* Aisling didn't care much for the thought.

"And don't go getting ideas. Your mission is to keep a low profile. Get that machine to Hermann in Thun as quickly as you can. We'll keep S.K.U.N.K. occupied with us. Where did I put the tickets, Florence?"

"In the second drawer from the left in front of you."

"Ah, there they are. The boy scouts are right—you should always be prepared. You're not a boy scout, are you?"

"No." Aisling grinned. "Nor a girl guide either."

"Pity."

Aisling waited.

"Where was I? Ah yes. This..." he handed her a ticket, "is a single from Paris to Basel. And this..." he handed her another one, "is from Basel to Thun. Here's a map of how to get to Hermann's house. Memorize it and destroy it."

"Jeeps."

"Does that benighted educational establishment you call a school teach you enough French to find the way to the railway station?"

"Er, yes." Aisling hoped so, anyway.

"Good. Now see if the coast is clear."

She looked through the periscope. Apart from a group of elderly Frenchmen playing bowls under the street lamps in the middle of the square, it was deserted. "It's okay, I think."

Florence helped her into her anorak and handed her a holdall and a plastic bag. "I've made you some sandwiches. Just in case you get hungry." She gave Aisling a quick peck on the cheek, peered through the peephole at the back of the tanker, satisfied herself that no-one was watching and let her out. "Good luck. Remember to keep warm and eat properly."

Aisling waved goodbye and dodged behind one of the broad-trunked trees. She walked as casually as possible to the nearest side street. None of the men in the centre of the square looked up. She turned: John Smith and Dermot were coming out of the Café des Amis at the other side of the square. She shrank into the shadows and watched them walk back to the tanker. They seemed to be chatting amicably enough. They got into the cab and, a minute later, the engine coughed into life and the tanker moved off. Aisling couldn't see which one of them was driving. She hoped it was Dermot.

She was just about to move when she heard

the sound of another engine. A small French car left the kerb and followed the tanker. Two people were in it: from where she was standing, she couldn't be certain if they were the window cleaner and the little old lady, but they certainly looked like them. She shivered. She wondered if Seamus knew they were following him. It was certainly as well he'd got his machine out when he did.

She noticed a newspaper kiosk further down the road. She picked up her bag and walked towards it. *Aisling Daly, multi-lingual traveller, converses with the natives,* she thought wryly.

"Où est la gare?" she asked in her best French accent.

The stout lady behind the counter seemed to understand. "Ce n'est pas loin, ma petite," she answered. "Tu-tournes-à-gauche-et-puis-tu-prends-la-première-rue-à-droite-et-tu-continues-tout-droit-jusqu'à-ce-que-tu-vois-la-gare-en-face. C'est bien facile."

Madame Colombe hadn't prepared her for this. Aisling's face fell.

The lady leaned her ample bosom on a copy of *Paris Match* and peered down at her over the counter. She smiled, showing irregular grey teeth with a large gap on the right side. "A

gauche," she said, very slowly and very loudly.
Aisling stepped back a pace. The lady pointed
down a side-street on the left. "Puis à droite."
She indicated right. "Puis tout droit." Her hand
moved away from her bosom in a straight line
until she could reach no further. "Et puis, tu y
es!" She smiled her gap-toothed smile.

"Merci, Madame." Hoping she'd understood
correctly, Aisling set off down the street on the
left.

12
Cornered

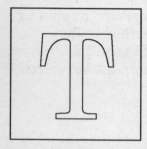

he station was bleak and cold. Beyond the platform lights, the night sky was pitch black and starless. Aisling shivered and shrank into a doorway. Behind her, a poster exhorted the public: *Visitez l'Angleterre!* and showed a faded grey photo of the Blackpool tower. The station smelt foreign: a funny mixture of diesel oil and garlic and strong cigarettes. The only other passengers on the platform were a nun with a black leather suitcase, two young girls with rucksacks on their backs, an elderly couple, and three men in berets talking together in a huddle at the far end. Aisling didn't trust the three men. Whatever happened, she'd better make sure she didn't get into the same compartment as they did. She kept looking round at the ticket office, half-expecting to see Shavitov or Lerntowski coming through the barrier. She wished the train would come.

Her holdall was heavy. She put it on the ground between her feet and rested the plastic bag with the sandwiches on top of it. The holdall wobbled and then straightened itself again. Its canvas squeaked.

When the train finally arrived, it was only half full. Aisling found an empty compartment and sat down beside the window. She was about to put the holdall under the seat when it squeaked again. It can't be the canvas, she thought. She opened it carefully. There, curled up on one of Florence's nighties, with a grin on his bewhiskered face as if he'd just won a year's supply of raw liver, was Mulligan.

"What on earth are you doing here?" she whispered. Surely Florence wouldn't have put him in the bag? He must have jumped in when she wasn't looking, she thought. But, however he had got there, it was good to have him with her. She put a hand into the holdall and stroked his back. He rubbed the side of his chin against her fingers and purred loudly.

"Shh!" Aisling saw a movement in the corridor. "Someone's coming. Go to sleep!"

She closed the zip again and placed the bag

gently on the floor just as the elderly couple she had seen on the platform came into the compartment. They smiled at her, put their cases and a string bag bulging with fruit and vegetables on the rack above their heads and laid a wicker basket on the seat directly opposite Aisling. She hoped it didn't contain another cat.

They smiled at her again, settled themselves comfortably and started chatting together, but their French was too fast for Aisling to catch more than an odd word or two. She was forced to admit that Madame Colombe had been right and she should have worked harder at French. She certainly would when she got home. If she got home. S.K.U.N.K. seemed to be a very powerful organisation: she wondered unhappily if Seamus's plan would fool them after all.

She turned her attention back to the elderly couple.. At least they couldn't be S.K.U.N.K. agents. She grinned at the thought. They looked rather sweet, like a pair of doting grandparents. They were holding hands, she noticed. It was funny seeing people so old holding hands, but rather nice all the same. Maybe they were going to visit their grandchildren in Switzerland: maybe their family had had to escape from France during the war because of the Nazis: *Aisling Daly, resistance heroine, leads a party of French refugees over the Alps to safety...*

A whistle blew and the train started to move off. A few minutes later, the nun came into the compartment and sat in the corridor seat on Aisling's side. She took out her rosary beads. The low murmur of prayer, even in a foreign language, was reassuring. S.K.U.N.K. would surely not start anything now, not with three witnesses in her compartment. Although—she remembered the episode on the boat—they could be so plausible and no-one had helped her then.

She stared worriedly out of the window. For the most part there was nothing to see but the reflection of the brightly-lit compartment, though now and again the lights of a house or a town would twinkle in the distance. Soon snow started to fall and broad flakes swirled up against the window, suffocating the train in a white cocoon.

The old lady opposite opened her basket. It contained a picnic. At least that was one danger averted, Aisling thought. She took out two napkins and handed one to her husband: the other she spread neatly over her broad lap. She then took two chunky, mouth-watering sandwiches made out of sections of French loaf from the basket, gave one to her husband, hesitated, offered the other to the nun who refused with a gentle smile, and then offered it to Aisling. She shook her head and muttered "Non, merci."

The holdall between her legs started to twitch. She quickly opened the plastic bag Florence had given her. Inside were enough sandwiches to feed an army. *French train breaks down on Swiss border. Snow drifts hamper rescue workers. "If it hadn't been for the extra food provided by Irish girl, Aisling Daly, hundreds would have died of starvation," claims survivor.* She grinned.

Concealing a meat sandwich in her hand, she pretended to be looking for something in her holdall. Mulligan wolfed the sandwich instantly. Aisling fed him four more, dreading to think what Florence's nightie must be like by now, considering his eating habits. Fortunately, the other three didn't seem to notice what she was doing or, if they did, they must have put it down to some strange foreign custom and were too polite to comment on it.

The noise of the wheels changed as the train slowed down. They must be approaching a station, Aisling thought. She tried to visualize the map: it was probably Belfort, the last French town before the border. The customs men would probably check their passports here.

Passports! She felt the blood leave her face. Boy scouts indeed—that was something Seamus hadn't thought of. What on earth was she to do?

She glanced worriedly at the bag on the floor. At least Mulligan appeared to have gone back to sleep. Though it was probably illegal to smuggle cats into Switzerland too. *Promising young Irish scholar gets ten years in French jail...*

She forced herself to stay calm. Picking up the bag as casually as possible, she squeezed past the nun and locked herself into the toilet at the end of the corridor.

She felt the train stop. Someone shouted something outside on the platform. At the other side of the door, people appeared to be arguing. The frosted glass of the toilet window prevented her from seeing what was going on, but it also, she thought with gratitude, meant that no-one would see her either. She opened the holdall and took Mulligan onto her lap where he kneaded his claws into her knees and rubbed his head up against her stomach. She hugged him tightly.

Finally, the train shuddered and moved off again. Aisling waited until the lights from the station had disappeared and there was only blackness outside her window again. Then, putting Mulligan back into the bag, she ventured out into the corridor.

She returned to the compartment. The elderly couple had left, but the nun was still there. She looked up from her prayer book as Aisling came in and smiled. Aisling smiled back and took her seat by the window again. She wondered how to ask in French if the customs officials had been, but decided it was too complicated. She'd just have to hope for the best.

They had to pass through a range of mountains before they reached Basel—the Juras, she thought—but it couldn't be long now. She gazed out at the flakes of snow floating in the light of the carriage window: they whirled and eddied and danced hypnotically. Despite the snow, the compartment was roasting hot. Aisling's head drooped.

***

A shrill whistle woke her. At first she couldn't remember where she was. She seemed to be in a very small box with a great crowd of people. Then the click of the wheels reminded her: she was on the train to Switzerland. But what on earth was happening? She blinked.

A small fat man wearing a dark uniform with a peaked cap and epaulettes was blocking the door into the corridor. A customs official! She shrank back into the corner in horror.

But the customs man wasn't interested in her. A grey flannel petticoat, various pairs of thick knitted stockings and two pairs of the type of bloomers she'd once seen on her granny's washing line, were scattered higgledy-piggledy over the free seats in the compartment. The nun herself was standing looking down at her case. Her face was white apart from a few dark hairs which showed up starkly on her upper lip. In the bottom of her suitcase were—Aisling looked in disbelief—layers of bank notes!

Aisling stared from the money to the nun. The whistle sounded again. She realized it was the customs man who was blowing it.

Footsteps sounded in the corridor. A second customs officer appeared at the door. There was a short conversation between them, the first officer picked up the suitcase, stuffed the scattered underwear back into it and closed the lid, and then both officers escorted the nun from the compartment. She didn't say a word.

Aisling watched as the second officer pulled the door closed and then let out her breath in a long sigh. She couldn't believe her luck. She opened her bag and stroked Mulligan. "Good boy," she whispered. "We ought to be safe now. I'll let you out when we get to Basel." Mulligan purred.

***

A shadow fell across the window to the corridor. The door opened again. Two men, one fat, one thin, came into the compartment. Aisling zipped the bag shut and jumped to her feet: it was Shavitov and Lerntowski themselves!

"Good evenink, girl." The fat man, Shavitov, gave an evil grin. "Ve are betting you are surprised to see us, no?"

Yes, Aisling agreed silently, her mind racing. Where on earth had they suddenly come from? They must have been on the boat and followed the tanker after all. And seen her get onto the train. Or had John Smith found a way to tell them where she was?

"You theenk how hav ve found you, yes?"

asked Shavitov, as if reading her thoughts. "You theenk you are clevair to escape from tanker and take train. But ve are clevairer still, no? Your friend, he drives tanker to us. Ve find no girl, no machine. Vere have grandpappy sent girl and machine? Ve theenk train. Ve drive to Belfort, very queek. And so..." He raised his hands theatrically and smiled again. Aisling wished he wouldn't; it sent chills down her back.

Lerntowski walked past his friend and sat down opposite her. He took his hat off, placed it squarely on his knees and stared morosely through the compartment window.

Shavitov laid a podgy hand on Aisling's shoulder and pressed her back into her seat. She tried to resist, but it was like being squashed by a human car-crusher. Shavitov eased his large form into the seat next to her. He thrust his broad face with its layers of wobbling chins right up to her. He had bad breath, Aisling noticed.

"So," said Shavitov. "Ve are here and you are here, no? And you vill be good girl and give us ze machine, yes?"

"No," said Aisling, her heart thudding. She backed away as far as possible, but was hampered by the window behind her.

Shavitov smiled again. What d'you bet he says we have ways of making you talk? Aisling asked herself.

"Ve do not need vays of making you talk." Shavitov again seemed to have read her thoughts. "Ve know you have grandaddy's machine. Ve take it now, yes?" He reached for the bag between her feet.

She gripped the bag tightly between her legs and grabbed the handle with both hands. The fat man laughed.

"You theenk you are stronk, no? But Shavitov is stronker. You vill see."

He put his huge paw across Aisling's two hands and gently loosened her fingers. He did it quite effortlessly, but she felt as if her fingers were being prised apart by a steel claw. Shavitov put his right arm across her chest, pinning her to the back of the seat. With his left hand he picked up the bag and placed it on his vast lap. Aisling tried to struggle, but it was as if a ten-ton bar of concrete had fallen from the roof of the train and was crushing her into the corner. She looked desperately at Lerntowski. Lerntowski continued to stare glumly out into the snow-flecked circle of light outside the train window.

Still grinning at Aisling, Shavitov felt for the

zip of the bag with his left hand. Aisling held her breath. Shavitov pulled the zip open.

He leered into Aisling's face. "You zought you could save ze vorrld, no?" he hissed through blackened teeth. "But nobody cans. S.K.U.N.K. has... how you say...? ze tramp card."

"Tramp card?" repeated Aisling, baffled.

Shavitov shook his head. "Tramp, no," he said sadly. Then his eyes lit up. "Trump, yes? Ve hav ze ace of spades. Ve keeps ze hole up zere open until your government gives us everyzink ve vants, no?"

Yes, Aisling thought. If nobody could close up the ozone hole, S.K.U.N.K. would have the world at its mercy.

Suddenly Shavitov sneezed. His face went purple. He threw the bag on the floor (fortunately it landed right side up) and tore at the neck of his jumper. Sneeze followed sneeze in rapid succession - it was almost as if the part of the Cardinal's curse quoted by Florence in Châlons-sur-Marne had come home to roost.

"Cats!!!" he screamed, jumping up and clawing at the window. "I needs air! Zere ees a cat in zees train! I must get air!!!"

Aisling saw her chance. Gathering up the bag with Mulligan still in it, she charged Shavitov so that he fell, sneezing, on to

Lerntowski, crushing the latter like a crumpled dummy across the seat opposite. She escaped into the corridor.

There was a crowd of people outside, standing with their luggage. "Help!" she shouted at the nearest man. "There's a man sick in there! He needs help!"

"Comment?"

"Wie bitte?"

"Ein Kranker?"

"Un malade?"

And, as she'd hoped, the whole crowd moved into the compartment, jamming the doorway, to see if they could help. That should hold Lerntowski up a bit, she thought.

She raced along the corridor, dodging between people, squeezing past suitcases, clutching the bag holding Mulligan to her chest and using it, when necessary, as a battering ram. No doubt she was doing little for the reputation of Irish youth, but she didn't care. Outside the train, lights flashed by—street lights. They must be in Basel already. If she could just keep ahead of the S.K.U.N.K. agents until the train stopped and get onto the platform without being seen, she might escape yet.

She continued down the corridor as fast as

she could, pushing through people waiting to get off, heading always towards the front of the train. When it finally drew to a halt, she was in the corridor of the first carriage, just behind the engine. The door was blocked by a fat lady and her husband. The man descended first and the fat lady passed him their suitcases. They seemed never-ending. Then the man helped the lady down the steps. Aisling fumed with impatience. At last the doorway was free and she could jump down herself.

She followed the fat lady down the platform and tried to dodge past her. She dodged back again almost immediately. She had seen a face she recognized at the barrier: the little old lady from the car ferry was waiting for her! If she was here, then the window cleaner was probably with her.

She hid behind a pillar. She had to find a way of getting off the platform without being seen. She looked behind her. There was no sign of either Lerntowski or Shavitov yet, but they couldn't be far behind.

She closed her eyes and prayed fervently. If ever she needed help, it was now.

And, miraculously it seemed, help was there. Coming along the platform, laughing and messing and jostling one another, was an unruly crowd of children: the school party which had helped her get onto the boat at Rosslare.

"Hey!" she hissed as the group she knew passed the pillar. "Patrick, Helen! Over here!"

The small boy with glasses heard her. "What are you doing here? I thought you were going to France?"

"Did I say that? I meant Switzerland. My Dad's in Basel. But I've just seen my stepfather. He must have followed me and he's over there, waiting for me. He'll kill me if he catches me, and he's sure to see me if I go any further."

"We'll get you through." They crowded round her as before and escorted her through the people waiting at the barrier. She thought she'd got away with it again. Then:

"There she is! With these bleeding school kids!" It was the window cleaner's voice.

"Run!" urged the boy from Cork.

Aisling ran towards the station exit. She was aware of a scuffle behind her, heard the window cleaner swearing and the worried voice of the teacher trying to control his party who appeared, from the noise behind her, to have started a fight in the station, and then she had reached the steps to the street.

13
Basel

isling found herself in a large square. The snow had stopped falling but it still lay white and unblemished on the house tops, on parked cars, on tram shelters and kiosks. The headlights of the few cars about so early in the morning sparkled in the frosty air; a tram passed like a glowworm.

She looked behind: no one was following her. Yet.

She crossed the road and dived into the tunnel of a pedestrian subway. She surfaced again at the entrance to a small park whose bushes, laden with snow and looking as if they'd come straight out of a Christmas card, offered a place to hide and get her breath back.

She slipped into the park, taking care to walk on snow that had already been trodden on so that her footprints didn't show. Once she was well away from the entrance, she left the path, jumping as far across the snow as possible and then smoothing her footsteps out behind her. As the park was not particularly well lit, she didn't think anybody would notice them. She hid behind a bush and let Mulligan out of the holdall.

He twined himself gratefully round her legs, making a noise like a bee trapped in a microphone, and then disappeared into the bushes. There was a sound of scratching and he came out again. He lifted one front paw out of the snow, licked it dry, lifted the other, licked it dry, lifted the first, regarded it with disgust and jumped back into the bag.

Aisling looked carefully through the bushes to see if she'd been followed. A loud miaow from behind her made her jump. Mulligan was sniffing the crumbs at the bottom of the bag. He looked up and miaowed hungrily again.

"I can't help you," she whispered. "I left the sandwiches on the train. Just be quiet, will you? Anyone could hear."

There was a noise on the path. She peered through the bushes again. A boy passed under the lamp opposite: he was walking slowly and examining the snow on either side of the path very carefully. Aisling held her breath.

Then Mulligan miaowed again.

Aisling turned in horror. She pushed him, none too gently, back down into the bottom of the bag and zipped it closed. He miaowed even louder, disgusted at such treatment. The sound was quite audible, even through the canvas. She took off her anorak and threw it over the bag; then she crouched over it herself, shielding it with her body, making shushing noises and trying to keep Mulligan quiet. It was like trying to smother an alarm clock.

There was a crash of twigs and the boy was standing next to her. Aisling picked up the bag and stood up, ready to run.

The boy grabbed her arm. "Wait! I'm Peter. I've come to help you."

"You've got the wrong person." Aisling tried to pull her arm away. "Let me go!"

He turned her towards him, his face anxious. He almost shook her. "Be sensible! There's not much time. They could be here any moment. I'm Peter Souter. My father is Seamus's friend, Hermann. You've got to trust me."

Aisling hesitated.

"Look. Seamus told us that he might have to send his part of Dad's machine by train. I was to keep a look out at the station in case anyone came through. I saw the school children trip up the man with the cap and Frau Schultz who was with him and then I saw you run down the steps. So I knew you must be the person Seamus sent. I am right, aren't I? You do have Seamus's part for Dad's machine?"

"I don't know what you're talking about."

"Du liebe Zeit!" The boy looked at her in exasperation. Another miaow came from the holdall. "Is that Mulligan you've got in there? If it is, he knows me."

Aisling let him take the bag and open it. Mulligan leapt out immediately and purred around him like a kettle over a high flame, rubbing his head against the boy's chin and kneading his claws into his coat. "Grüssti, Liebling!" The boy stroked Mulligan's thick fur. He looked up at Aisling. "It's so nice to see him again."

"How do you know Mulligan?"

"I used to play with him when we visited Seamus."

"When was that?"

"A year or two ago." Peter put Mulligan gently back into the bag. "But we haven't time to talk now. We must hurry. I shall bring you to Tante Margarethe in the Clarastrasse. And then we can plan what to do."

Aisling thought of her instructions to take the next train to Thun. On the other hand, there was no point in going back to the station to be caught. If the window cleaner and Frau Schultz, or whatever the old woman was called, were still there, there was no way she'd get on the train safely. And, if she didn't get on the train, what was she going to do all night in a strange city, with no money, where she didn't know a soul and couldn't even speak the language? She admitted to herself that she was cold, tired, frightened and hungry and decided wearily to trust Peter. For the moment at least.

They left the park by its other exit and kept to narrow, snow-covered back streets until they were sure no one was following them. Eventually they came to another square. Here they boarded the front half of one of the weird Swiss tramcars which Aisling thought looked as if they'd been sliced in two with the top deck strung on behind the bottom one like jointed mechanical caterpillars. They travelled in it along streets of well-kept houses with carved wooden shutters and imposing front doors, houses which looked solid and prosperous and sure of themselves compared to the tall narrow French houses of the day before, which had seemed to lean up against each other for protection. They passed illuminated shop fronts with signs often in both French and German, old churches and medieval buildings, flagposts bearing the white cross of Switzerland against a red background, and finally they crossed the Rhine itself, a huge river looking dirty and grey under the street lamps from the bridge.

Peter's aunt was waiting for them in her tiny modern flat. She was a small woman with greying hair drawn tightly back in a bun. She kissed Aisling warmly and showed her into a comfortable sitting room full of books, pictures and plants. Aisling relaxed: Tante Margarethe just couldn't be a S.K.U.N.K. agent; she was far too nice. She sank down onto the sofa. It was marvellous to feel that someone else had taken over and could make the decisions and look after things.

She watched as Tante Margarethe fed Mulligan and then allowed herself to be led to the bathroom, took a shower at Tante Margarethe's suggestion, came back, drank the bowl of hot chocolate waiting for her and then collapsed, exhausted, on to the bed in Tante Margarethe's spare room, snuggling under the enormous white duvet without even noticing the sandwich crumbs in the old-fashioned nightie Florence had packed for her. She thought about Seamus and Florence: had they been captured as Shavitov had claimed or was it just a bluff? Shavitov had said "their friend" had driven the tanker to them. That must mean that John Smith was working for S.K.U.N.K. after all. So much for Florence's intuition.

She tried to worry about what would happen to Seamus and Florence and Dermot, if Shavitov had been telling the truth, but she was far too tired...

***

The next thing she knew, it was morning and Peter was shaking her awake. A breakfast of fresh crispy rolls, butter, raspberry jam and piping hot coffee made her almost feel that she could face the problems of S.K.U.N.K. again, which was just as well.

Peter brought the subject up as soon as she sat down. "Father wants you to bring him Seamus's part as soon as possible. His machine is almost finished; all the other parts are ready. The sooner we can try it out, the better."

"Do you think it will be able to close the ozone hole?"

Peter shrugged. "We don't know. It hasn't

been tried yet."

"We must hope," said Tante Margarethe. "What is it your poet says? Hope springs eternal in the human backbone?"

"Something like that," Aisling agreed, trying to hide a grin.

She felt the small rectangular box in the pouch on her belt and remembered that there was nothing to smile about. Seamus's machine had to be got to Hermann or the world would be destroyed by ultra-violet rays. *Aisling Daly saves mankind*. She wished it was someone else.

"Father is no longer in Thun," Peter explained. "He is holding a meeting of all the inventors at a safe house in Zurich. He guessed what S.K.U.N.K. was doing and summoned them all some time ago. Lin Chin Po from Asia, Chrysler III from North America, Kurote from Africa, Coolihan from Australasia and Calderon from South America have all arrived, but Seamus didn't come."

"He came as soon as he heard," said Aisling. "Or at least, the very next day."

"Then perhaps S.K.U.N.K. cut into the message," suggested Tante Margarethe. "Hermann must have surprised them by walking so fast. They must have thought they could put a pin in our wheels by stopping Seamus from getting here. I gather you had some mischief?"

Aisling grinned. Mischief was a good word. She told them what had happened since they'd left home.

"So," said Tante Margarethe. "That is interesting. So Seamus is proposing to attack S.K.U.N.K. directly. I hope he is careful but at least Florence is there to keep a glance on him. If he has not yet been caught—and I would not believe what that Shavitov tells you—then he may have a possibility. We do not think S.K.U.N.K. knows that Hermann and the others are in Zurich. They were still watching the house near Thun yesterday where Hermann has left a sitting hen."

"Duck," corrected Peter.

"Don't you mean he's using the house as a blind?" suggested Aisling, trying not to smile.

"Blind? Shutter? What does it matter?" asked Tante Margarethe impatiently. "Now, pay attention. I have been thinking and I have come down with a plan. Peter will take Seamus's machine to his father as he knows where to find him and S.K.U.N.K. will be peeking for you and will not suspect him. This is how we will do it: we will all go off together, now, in my car (it is only a sausage, but it will do)..."

"Banger?" suggested Aisling.

Tante Margarethe looked at her. "Please do not interrupt. This is grave."

"Sorry."

"We will all go off in my car, as I said, and we will no doubt be followed. I shall drive south and let you out at the next station after Basel. We will time it so that you will just trap the train. We hope that S.K.U.N.K. will follow you. You will be the red kipper."

"Herring," Peter corrected.

Tante Margarethe ignored him. "We will take my dressmaker's dummy," she gestured towards a wickerwork frame in the shape of a human being which was standing in a corner of the room. "We will dress it in Peter's clothes and they will think it is Peter. Peter will hide in the car. After you take the train, Aisling, I shall bring Peter to the house of a friend who will help him to get to Zurich. He will get out of the car without anyone seeing and S.K.U.N.K. will think he is the dummy and still in the car. Then I will lead any S.K.U.N.K. persons who have not followed you and are still on my behind on a wild swan chase back to Basel."

This time Aisling didn't bother to correct her.

She looked from Peter to his aunt thoughtfully. The plan might work. But it was one thing letting them help her to get the machine to Hermann; it was another to hand it over completely. She wondered if she ought to let it out of her sight.

There was a loud knocking at the flat door. The three of them looked at one another. Who could it be?

14
The Chase

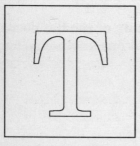ante Margarethe stood up. She pressed a button on a speaker by the side of the door. "Wer ist da?" she asked.

"Good morning, Madam," replied a voice which made Aisling drop her coffee cup with a clatter.

"Who is it?" whispered Peter.

"It's one of them!"

"I apologize for calling so early in the morning," John Smith's voice was as cheerful as ever. "But I was hoping to catch you before you leave." Aisling and Peter exchanged glances. How much did he know? "Can I interest you in a luxury German-language edition of our *Encyclopedia for the Expansion of Young Minds*?"

"No," said Tante Margarethe shortly.

"Goodbye."

"Ah don't be hasty now, Madam. I'm sure you are a lady of culture and discernment. If you would only open the door and take just one glance at this marvellous work of reference, I'm certain you won't be able to resist it."

Tante Margarethe looked questioningly at Aisling. She shook her head violently.

"Goodbye," Tante Margarethe said again through the speaker.

"Did you know," John Smith continued unperturbed, "that the laws of hospitality in the Arab world compel every Bedouin (Volume 2, D for Deserts) to take a stranger into his tent even if it is his worst enemy and not a friend in disguise? Aha, I thought you didn't."

"Will you please leave," said Tante Margarethe. "I am going to call the police."

"Oh dear." John Smith sighed. "I often think," he said less cheerfully than usual, "that if everyone really took to heart the entry under T for Trust (Volume 10) or L for Love of Mankind (Volume 6), the world would be a better place and salesmen such as myself wouldn't have to work under such terrible conditions of mistrust, threats and persecution. You have no idea, Madam, how hard the life of a travelling salesman is."

"No doubt," said Tante Margarethe unsympathetically. "Go away."

There was a silence from the other side of the door. Then John Smith spoke again. "If you change your mind, Madam, and decide to buy one of these marvellous, indispensable, unique works of reference without which no home should be, here is my card." A slip of white card was pushed under the door. "You never know— perhaps your nephew or his Irish friend would like a set for Christmas. Au revoir."

Retreating steps sounded outside and then there was silence again. Tante Margarethe opened the door very carefully and looked out into the corridor. "He is gone," she said. "And good riddance to bad dustbins, I would say." She picked the card up from the floor. "John Smith," she read. "Encyclopedia salesman. TAKE CARE: THEY KNOW AISLING IS WITH YOU."

"And you think he is a S.K.U.N.K. person?" she asked Aisling.

"Yes. Shavitov admitted as much. Although Florence trusts him."

"I wonder how he knew you were here. Did he follow you from the station last night?"

"I don't think so. Shavitov said he'd driven the tanker straight to them, but he didn't say

where that was. I suppose it might have been
Basel. They might have seen Peter and me
coming here." The thought made her skin
prickle.

"Perhaps. And perhaps it was just
guesswork that made him come here," said
Tante Margarethe thoughtfully. "But we had
better get a flit on all the same. Are you willing
to be the red kipper, Aisling?"

"I suppose so." After all, if S.K.U.N.K. had
traced her to here, there was no point in trying
to go it alone. The only way to fool them now was
to do as Tante Margarethe suggested and let
Peter deliver Seamus's machine while she kept
the enemy busy following her for as long as
possible. She only hoped that, once they caught
her, they'd let her go again when they
discovered she hadn't got it any more. She
wished she could be more confident that they
would. Reluctantly, she unfastened the belt
and handed it to Peter.

"Good." Tante Margarethe fetched Aisling's
holdall from the bedroom, took her
dressmaker's dummy apart and packed it in the
holdall along with a spare coat and hat
belonging to Peter. She checked the corridor
again to see if the coast was clear and all three,
with Aisling holding Mulligan in her arms,

made a dash for the lift. Nobody tried to stop them.

Aisling expected John Smith or some of the other S.K.U.N.K. agents to be waiting for them in the garage in the basement—the sinking feeling in her stomach as the lift plunged downwards was not solely the effect of the change in altitude. She was relieved when they opened the lift doors and found nobody there.

They raced across the deserted garage to Tante Margarethe's tiny white Renault. Tante Margarethe squeezed herself into the front seat and threw the holdall down beside her, and Aisling and Peter (and Mulligan) piled into the back. Fortunately the car started first time. Tante Margarethe put her foot on the accelerator and they zoomed up the exit ramp and turned sharply right into the Clarastrasse.

Aisling looked back. A car, a black saloon, had followed them out of the garage and was close on their heels. A grey Volkswagen, which had been parked at the side of the road opposite the block of flats, pulled out and followed the saloon. Unfortunately, it was still too dark to see who was in either car, but she didn't believe that their presence in the Clarastrasse was a pure coincidence.

"There's two of them following us, I think,"

she reported.

"Good." Tante Margarethe sounded satisfied. "This is quite like old ages. Did you know, Aisling, that I was once a rally driver? I shall now pretend to scrape them off. Will you make sure we do not really lose them or our plan will go screwy."

The next half-hour was hair-raising. Tante Margarethe swerved down side streets, screeched round corners, whizzed round the same roundabout three times until Aisling was dizzy, skidded along narrow streets lined with walls of dirty snow abandoned by snowploughs in the night, smiled sweetly at any policemen she passed, avoided trams and other cars by the thickness of a coat of paint and finally reached the outskirts of town. Scrape them off was it, Aisling thought.

She had been watching the road behind them: apart from anything else, it was less nerve-wracking than looking ahead to see what Tante Margarethe was just about to miss next. No matter how she had dodged and swerved or how fast she had driven, the black saloon was always on their tail, with the grey Volkswagen not far behind.

Aisling shivered. Although it was getting lighter all the time, she still couldn't see the occupants of either car clearly but there were at least two people in the black saloon. She clutched Mulligan closer. He rubbed his head against her cheek and purred contentedly. If the two behind were Shavitov and Lerntowski, she thought, he might just save her again; but it was much more likely to be the window cleaner and the old lady, or John Smith and a friend, and it would be too much to hope for that any of them would be allergic to cats as well. Tante Margarethe's plan sounded okay in theory but being a red kipper in practice might not be such fun. *Mysterious death of Irish schoolgirl in Switzerland: the body of Aisling Daly, guarded by her faithful cat, was found yesterday on the train between Thun and Basel...* She squeezed Mulligan even tighter.

Something hit her behind her left ear. "Ouch!" she said. Something else whammed into Mulligan's rump. Mulligan decided that enough was enough and fled to the floor like a ferret down a burrow, digging his rear feet into Aisling's stomach to gain impetus for his dive.

"Will you please sit quiet, Aisling," snapped Tante Margarethe. "You are disturbing my compression."

"Concentration?" queried Aisling as she dodged a flailing arm. The tailor's dummy appeared to have come to life.

"Can't you control that thing?" she asked Peter bitterly as she dodged once again.

"Just one more minute. I'm almost finished."

Aisling squeezed herself into the furthest corner of the back seat and watched cautiously as Peter finished reassembling the dummy and buttoned it neatly into his winter coat.

"Now!" he told Tante Margarethe.

The car accelerated with a jerk and zoomed down a side road. It skidded and jarred over rutted snow and Aisling thought her last minute had come. *Schoolgirl found dead in snowdrift...* But Tante Margarethe kept control and she found herself breathing again. The saloon had been too close behind and had missed the turning; the grey Volkswagen skidded round the corner out of control and slid gently into the ditch.

"Good." Tante Margarethe glanced in her mirror. "We have wiped them away. Quick!"

Peter pulled his woollen hat over the dummy's head and set it up in the back seat beside Aisling. He put on the spare coat which had been in the holdall and crouched down at Aisling's feet. "Okay?" he asked.

"A great improvement."

"Pig," said Peter from the floor. He bashed

her hard on the shin.

Mulligan, finding it too crowded on the floor, jumped out of the way to land like a ton of concrete-lined fur on Aisling's knees. She dumped him unceremoniously in the now-empty holdall and closed the zip.

"Will you two stop making such a bat!" ordered Tante Margarethe. "Aisling! Can you see any notice of S.K.U.N.K.?"

Aisling had been trying to work out what she meant by bat. "Racket!" she exclaimed as realization hit her.

"No, S.K.U.N.K.," said Tante Margarethe patiently.

Aisling turned to look out of the window. The road behind them was empty. A thousand butterflies left her stomach in a swarm. The sun shone brighter. The day might turn out not so bad after all.

Tante Margarethe did not share her relief. "That is bad. We must find them again. What use is all these red haddocks if nobody sees them? We will go back to the main road and hook about until we shovel them up again."

Aisling sighed. And not only over Tante Margarethe's weird English. The butterflies, each weighted with a lump of lead, returned to her stomach. They became even heavier when

Tante Margarethe's plan succeeded and they picked up the two cars again.

"The train passes through at 8.49 exactly," stated Tante Margarethe as they approached a village south of Basel. "We will reach the station at 8.48. Perhaps S.K.U.N.K. will miss the train. If so, they will follow it to the next station and plank it there."

"Board," corrected Aisling weakly.

Tante Margarethe looked at her in surprise. The car swerved dangerously. "How can I be bored, Aisling?" she asked. "I have not had so much games in years!"

Aisling, looking back at the two cars, found it impossible to share her enthusiasm.

15
Hermann's Chalet

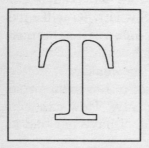ante Margarethe slowed down as they passed the station entrance and Aisling jumped out. She reached the platform just as the train came in; Swiss trains could obviously be depended on to arrive exactly on time. She looked back: there was no sign of anyone yet.

The train was crowded. The corridor was jammed with skiers and their equipment—rucksacks, anoraks, skis and sticks—but she managed to squeeze past and find a compartment with an empty seat. She sat down, her heart pounding. Had she done the right thing? She was sure Tante Margarethe and Peter were what they said they were, and yet...S.K.U.N.K. was clever. They *could* be S.K.U.N.K. agents.

For a moment she found herself actually hoping that they were. If S.K.U.N.K. had Seamus's machine, then nobody would bother chasing her. All she'd have to do now was find her way to the Irish Embassy—there'd have to be one in Switzerland somewhere—and they'd send her home. She gave herself a mental shake. Pull yourself together, child! as Seamus would say. The thought of Seamus cheered her up. She *had* to believe that his machine was being got safely to Hermann and that what she was doing on this train was necessary. *Aisling Daly saves the world!* she reminded herself.

The grin died on her face and the lead-weighted butterflies in her stomach started playing leap-frog with each other: outside, in the corridor, the window cleaner suddenly leered in at her. And behind him was the little old lady from the car ferry!

She looked desperately at the windows at the other side of the compartment. Beyond them, the snow-covered countryside flew past like a miniaturised, domesticated version of the Russian steppes but they were tightly closed against the cold air and there was no escape that way. She tried to ignore the two in the corridor. Surely they wouldn't attack her on a crowded train? But she remembered again how no one had helped her when she was being kidnapped on the boat. She clutched the holdall that contained Mulligan tightly for comfort.

There was a sudden movement in the corridor. She turned to face it. Were they going to rush her after all?

No. The little old lady had collapsed against the door of the compartment. The window cleaner was bending over her, a worried expression on his weasely face. "Are you all right, Mammy?" he asked loudly.

The little old lady groaned.

The window cleaner looked anxiously into the compartment. Immediately, a tall, bronzed young man sitting next to the door jumped to his feet. "Pray, let your mother have my chair," he suggested.

"Zank you, young man." The little old lady fluttered her eyelashes at him. "You are most kind."

The young man helped the window cleaner to bring the old lady into the compartment. "Now I will go to seek a doctor."

"No!" The window cleaner grasped his arm. "Sure, there's no need, so," he said hurriedly. "It's just one of her turns. She'll be all right now. You'll be all right now, Mammy, sure you will."

"Yes, son," whispered the little old lady with

a brave smile.

She settled herself comfortably in the seat. The window cleaner and the young man stood in the corridor. The window cleaner offered the young man a cigarette. Neither he nor the little old lady even looked at Aisling but, with one of them sitting just inside the door and the other one standing just outside it, she was now well and truly trapped. At least, she thought miserably, it proved which side Peter and Tante Margarethe were on.

As the train rushed on through the white Swiss countryside, Aisling tried to think calmly. There must be a way to escape! She became more and more desperate as the train passed through one station after another along the route: each time it slowed down, she thought this time she might have a chance, but nobody moved from her compartment, the little old lady still sat between herself and the door and the window cleaner stayed in the corridor. There was simply no possibility of making a run for it.

As they entered the suburbs of Thun the skiers stood up, gathered their gear together and put on their anoraks and caps. Aisling looked at the little old lady. She stared back, her eyes colder than ice behind her spectacles. The window cleaner moved closer to the door.

Aisling got to her feet. It was now or never. She gripped the holdall tightly.

Suddenly a man shouldered past the window cleaner and elbowed his way into the compartment. "Aha!" he said. "Devotees of the noble art of winter sports! Young minds just waiting to be expanded! Ladies and gentlemen, let me interest you in the incredible bargain I have here: twelve volumes of the *Encyclopedia for the Expansion of Young Minds* translated into French, German, Italian, Romance, Swiss-German, Dutch, Serbo-Croat... you name it, we have it! There are interesting articles on meteorology: did you know, for example, that snow forms directly from water vapour in the air when the temperature at the time of condensation is lower than zero degrees centigrade (thirty-two degrees Fahrenheit)? No, I thought not. Or geography? You could find out, just by turning a page, that the highest mountain in Switzerland, the Matterhorn, is a mere 14,688 feet (4,477 metres) compared with the 29,028 feet (8,848 metres) of Mount Everest! Or what about mechanics? Discover all you'll ever need to know about the working of your ski-lift and you'll never be stuck half-way up a mountain! There are even interesting facts about kidnapping, blackmail and murder which, would you believe, are on the increase in Switzerland even as I speak."

The skiers had listened to him at first, taken aback by his sudden intrusion and the self-confident way he announced himself and caught their attention; but by the time he was half-way through, they had already turned their backs on him and were finishing their preparations for departure.

John Smith turned to Aisling who had been standing, open-mouthed, watching the whole performance. "Nice to see you again, Aisling," he said brightly. "I knew from the first time I met you you had a mind interested in expanding itself. Let us leave these sport-obsessed yokels to their philistine pursuits."

Before she could blink, the encyclopedia salesman had grabbed her by the arm and dragged her down the corridor, out of the train and along the platform. The window cleaner and the little old lady hurried after them.

John Smith kept a tight grip on her arm as she felt for her ticket and gave it up. And then he steered her to the station exit. "Speed, as the poet said, is of the essence. We need a taxi." He beckoned to the first taxi in the rank outside the station, opened the door, pushed Aisling in and started to climb in himself.

The taxi suddenly shot off. The salesman grabbed the door, missed and fell in a heap in the snow, a look of incredulity on his face. Aisling grinned. What a stroke of luck!

The taxi driver turned round. "Hi, Ash! How's things?"

Aisling couldn't believe her eyes. "How did *you* get here?"

"We thought you might need a bit of help, isn't that right? So Seamus sent me down," Dermot explained. "I borrowed a taxi. I thought it might come in useful. It did too, wouldn't you say? That Smith man was right on your heels."

Aisling hadn't been sure if John Smith had been rescuing her from the window cleaner or helping him to catch her. But for the moment, it was a relief just to be safe. She sat back in the seat and settled the holdall comfortably on her knees. It started to leap about like a canvas jumping bean. She opened it cautiously. Mulligan leapt out, paused on the back of the driver's seat to give Aisling a filthy look as if to accuse her of having kept him incarcerated and starving for at least two days, and jumped down to crash onto Dermot's knees. The taxi swerved violently.

"Holy catfish!" Dermot grasped the wheel

and brought them back onto the road. "Get a grip on yourself, Mulligan. You scared me half to death there, isn't that right?"

Mulligan stood on his back paws, put his front paws on Dermot's shoulders and rubbed his head affectionately along Dermot's chin. Then, shutting his eyes to narrow slits, he licked Dermot's nose.

"Get off, you great idiot!" Dermot pushed him down gently. "How can I drive with your great hairy mug in my face? You stay there and behave yourself, isn't that right?"

Mulligan obeyed. He stretched right across Dermot so that his nose was over the gear lever and his tail hanging down beside the door, gave a huge sigh, put his head on his paws and lay motionless.

"Are Seamus and Florence all right?" asked Aisling. "Did S.K.U.N.K. capture the tanker? How did you escape?"

"Hold it!" Dermot grinned. "First, who told you S.K.U.N.K. had caught us?"

"Lerntowski and Shavitov. They almost got me on the train to Basel after I left you."

"They did, did they?" Dermot stroked Mulligan's head with one hand and steered the taxi skilfully round a sharp bend with the other. "And you believed them, isn't that right?"

"Well. Yes."

"Which just goes to show." Dermot sighed at the gullibility of mankind.

"You mean you weren't caught?"

"What do you think?" asked Dermot scornfully. "Your friend John Smith did his best, mind you. But I realized what he was up to and ditched him in time, isn't that right? I pushed him out of the driving cab onto the road. You should have seen his face, Ash. Boy, you should have seen his face."

Aisling, remembering John Smith falling into the snowdrift back at the station, almost began to feel sorry for him. "So Seamus and Florence are safe, then?" she asked again. "Are we going to them now?"

"Sure we are, Ash. They're waiting for us at Hermann's chalet, just ahead. We'll be there any minute now, isn't that right? Hold on, we leave the main road here."

Aisling held on. Dermot's driving was even more hair-raising than Tante Margarethe's had been: they swerved from one side of the narrow road to the other with the rear wheels spinning to get a grip on the snow-covered surface. She caught a glimpse of a lake on her right, and then a house appeared ahead, a low wooden chalet with a steep snow-covered roof and a verandah facing them above the broad entrance door.

As the taxi skidded to a halt, Aisling realized something was missing. "Where's the tanker?" she asked. "I don't see it."

"Behind the house," said Dermot. "Hermann thought it best to keep it hidden, isn't that right?"

Aisling wasn't sure. She remembered what Peter had told her: Hermann ought to have been in Zurich. She looked at the chalet again. Although the shutters were open and a path had been cleared from the road to the massive front door, it seemed completely deserted. "Did Hermann send you to meet me off the train?" she asked thoughtfully.

Dermot picked up Mulligan and got out of the taxi. "Sure," he said. "Come on now. Let's get Seamus's machine safely into the house, isn't that right?"

He waited for her at the door, his curly hair escaping from under his taxi-driver's cap, his *Health is Wealth* sweatshirt visible beneath his uniform jacket. His face wore its usual zany grin and Mulligan was sprawled trustingly over his shoulder. He had to be a friend.

"Come on, Ash. What's the matter with you? You're keeping Mulligan from his dinner, isn't

that right? Not to mention the fact that a man
could freeze to death out here."

Aisling picked up her bag and followed him.
No doubt Seamus would explain everything
when they got inside.

Dermot tried the door handle. The door was
locked.

Aisling struggled against a growing feeling
of suspicion. Were they walking into a trap? She
glanced round nervously, looking for
S.K.U.N.K. agents, but no matter how hard she
looked, she couldn't see anyone.

Dermot knocked at the door. There was no
answer. He muttered something and then
trudged through the knee-high snow around
the house, trying each window in turn. Aisling
followed him, becoming more and more
anxious. Something was obviously very wrong.

A small window at the back of the chalet was
unlatched. Dermot looked at it thoughtfully.
"Slim as I am, Ash old girl, I won't get through
there. I'll give you a leg up and you can open the
front door to me, isn't that right?"

Aisling hesitated. "Are you sure we're not
walking into a trap? It seems very fishy that
nobody's here." A thought struck her. "The
tanker's gone too. You said it was round the
back."

"They must have decided to go off somewhere without waiting for us. If we ever get in, we'll probably find a note or something. Are you going to try or do we stand here all day? My feet are beginning to get wet."

He lifted her up until she could reach the window and she struggled through it to find herself in a small cloakroom. She listened: there was no sound from the house. *Mysterious disappearance of Irish schoolgirl in Switzerland*, she thought, trying to smile. She opened the door and went into the entrance hall. To her left was a flight of smooth polished wooden stairs, to her right a large comfortable-looking sitting room and, beyond the stairs, another open door revealed a kitchen. Straight ahead of her was the front door.

She jumped as Dermot knocked again, loud enough to start an avalanche in the mountains. "Come on, Ash!" His voice was muffled by the sturdy door. "It's cold out here, isn't that right?"

She pulled back the bolt and opened the door. Dermot came in and stamped the snow off his boots. Mulligan dived from his shoulder, skidded on the polished parquet floor, picked himself up and headed unerringly for the kitchen. Aisling saw him crash to a stop in front of the fridge. "Maybe we should feed Mulligan before we look for a message," she suggested. "He hasn't had anything to eat since breakfast."

Dermot grinned. "Suffering catfish!" he exclaimed. "Or suffering cats, anyway, isn't that right? You'd better see what's in that fridge before he starves to death before your eyes."

Mulligan collapsed on to the kitchen floor, stretched out full length with his nose inches from the fridge door. He did indeed look on the point of death. Aisling pushed him sideways, grabbed the first thing she saw (a piece of cold chicken), dropped it on the floor and removed her hand, just in time, as Mulligan pounced like a starving wolf on a paralysed rabbit. She looked back at Dermot with a smile.

The smile froze on her face.

Dermot smiled back. "Seamus always did say he never knew a cat fonder of its stomach than that animated food processor, isn't that right?"

Aisling didn't reply. She was staring past Dermot at the two people standing behind him.

16
Treachery

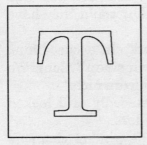

he window cleaner and the little old lady unbuttoned their coats, removed their hats, shook the snow from them and smiled at Aisling. Nastily.

Aisling vaulted over Mulligan, pulled the window open and scrambled up onto the sill.

"I vould not be doing zat if I vas you, yes?" Aisling felt each hair on her head stand up individually. She looked down. Shavitov was standing just beneath her and behind Shavitov, keeping out of the way of any drips from the overhanging chalet roof and with his feet nicely dry in the footprints trodden earlier by Dermot and herself, was Lerntowski.

As Aisling wondered whether to risk jumping and trying to run for it, she felt a hand on her arm. "Come on, kid. Down."

The window cleaner pulled her from the window and dragged her into the sitting room where Dermot and the little old lady were waiting. Dermot of all people! He'd seemed so harmless. And Florence and Seamus had trusted him completely. How could they have been so wrong?

"You lousy rotten traitor!" she accused him. "You must have been on their side all along! We trusted you. I thought you were nice."

Dermot grinned shamefacedly and looked away, shrugging his shoulders.

She tried to get out of the window cleaner's grasp. He laughed and twisted her arm as he'd done on the boat. "Go on," he encouraged her. "Try to escape. I've a lot, like, to get even with you for. You just try to get away and, sure as my name's Pat Flaherty, I'll break your bleeding arm."

"Enough!"

Aisling looked up in surprise at the strange, high-pitched voice. Lerntowski had come into the room and was standing at the window staring out at the snow. He didn't turn round, but she was sure it was he who had spoken. The window cleaner let go of her immediately. "Okay, okay," he grumbled, flashing Lerntowski a glance of what looked like hatred.

Aisling rubbed her arm and moved a step away. Lerntowski was at the window, Shavitov had followed her in to the room and was now between her and the door, and the little old lady and the window cleaner were standing by, both watching her closely: she was trapped. She had never felt more alone: even Mulligan had deserted her. *Corpse of Irish schoolgirl found in Swiss chalet*, she thought miserably. Or would they throw her in the lake?

There was a sound in the hall: someone had opened the front door. Aisling looked up hopefully. Had Hermann come home? Or was it Tante Margarethe or Peter? "Look out!" she yelled. "S.K.U.N.K.'s in here!"

The door opened, Shavitov moved aside and John Smith entered the room. For a moment, Aisling's spirits rose: perhaps he was against S.K.U.N.K. after all! He could have been trying to save her at the station just like he'd saved her on Killiney Hill. Why hadn't she trusted him instead of Dermot? If he tried to get her away from S.K.U.N.K. again, she'd be ready this time.

But he made no effort to help her. Worse, the others were obviously expecting him and showed no surprise at his appearance. "Afternoon," he said cheerfully. "It's a lovely day for a walk, although let's face it, I'm not as sold as some on the fitness bug." He winked at Dermot. "Still," he went on, removing his hat and gloves and dusting the snow from his shoulders, "I would have hated to have missed such a gathering of expanding and expanded minds. Pity none of you wants an encyclopedia. I'm tired of carting these things around. Unless I can interest Aisling in one at last?"

The window cleaner and Frau Schultz glared at him. "Vy did you not vait for us at ze station?" demanded Frau Schultz.

Aisling had been asking herself the same question.

John Smith grinned. "For the same reason our fitness freak didn't wait for me to get into his taxi, no doubt. And possibly for the same reason you drove past me on the road in such a hurry. I hope the Boss there appreciates the way we all rush about to fulfil his every command."

Lerntowski turned slowly round. He walked over to Aisling. "Give me the machine," he demanded in his prim, high-pitched voice.

She ignored him. "Why did you pretend to save me on the train?" she asked John Smith. "And on Dalkey Hill? If you're one of them, it doesn't make sense."

John Smith looked at her approvingly. "Perspicacious as ever, Aisling. We thought we had you fooled between us but you got it first time, even without the entry under T for Treachery to help you. I always knew you were a bright girl."

"Enough!" squeaked Lerntowski again.

John Smith waved a hand as if inviting Lerntowski to take over, settled himself comfortably in one of Hermann's armchairs and took out his pipe.

"I shall ask you once more," Lerntowski told Aisling. "Where is your godfather's machine?"

She looked into his tiny pig-like eyes. "I haven't got it."

Shavitov took a step towards her. "I help her memory, no?" he asked eagerly.

Lerntowski nodded. A huge arm came round Aisling's neck, half-throttling her.

"Search her first," ordered Lerntowski.

Shavitov's huge hand felt carefully through Aisling's clothes. "Eet ees ze truth. She has not got eet."

Lerntowski's small eyes grew even smaller, his mouth became even thinner, his face more rat-like, but his voice remained the same: high and soft and sounding almost bored. "Where have you put it?"

"I don't know what you're talking about."

The arm around her throat tightened. She winced.

"I believe her," said John Smith conversationally from the armchair. He started to fill his pipe calmly from a pouch on his lap. "Seamus wouldn't have given it to a girl."

"Sure, and isn't it well for you?" sneered the window cleaner. "So you believe her, do you? Well, I don't. She's just a lying, snivelling young pup. Just you twist her arm a bit, like, Shavitov. She'll talk soon enough."

At that moment Mulligan, having finished the chicken, came sauntering into the room, wondering if anyone there could be persuaded to give him some more. He rubbed himself against the nearest legs: Shavitov's.

Shavitov gave a loud sneeze, released Aisling and clawed at his throat. Aisling ran for the door. Unfortunately Shavitov, gasping for air, got there first. She tried to struggle past him but it was like trying to push past an elephant into a mousehole. Shavitov squeezed out into the hallway and made for the front door and fresh air but, before Aisling could follow, she was grabbed once again by the window cleaner. Lerntowski snapped something in a foreign language but Shavitov was already out of earshot. Aisling saw him through the window writhing about in the snow like a stranded whale, sneezing and gasping for breath.

Lerntowski shut the sitting room door and turned the key. "What is it you Irish say?" he asked in his high-pitched voice. "There are more ways than one of killing a cat."

Aisling flinched. Dermot, she noticed, jumped too.

Lerntowski's impassive face showed a flash of interest. He looked calculatingly from Mulligan, who was now rubbing himself against Dermot, to Aisling. "I am not a violent man," he squeaked. "I, too, have a daughter. She is also fond of animals."

Aisling's blood ran cold. "Shoo, Mulligan!" she hissed. "Go away!" She struggled in the window cleaner's grasp but was held as helplessly as a rabbit in a snare.

Mulligan came over and rubbed hopefully against her leg.

Lerntowski turned to the little old lady and gave a command in the foreign language.

The little old lady smiled unpleasantly, opened the door and went out into the kitchen. Mulligan raced after her eagerly. Someone was going to give him his second course at last.

She returned with a large carving knife

which she laid on the arm of a chair. "Come, pussy!" she said.

Mulligan skidded back from the kitchen and ran up to her, his tail in the air. He balanced on his hind legs and begged. She picked him up and put him on the back of the chair. He stretched himself out, purring loudly, delighted to be the centre of attention.

The little old lady placed her left hand firmly across his back and picked up the knife in her right hand.

"No!" shouted Aisling and Dermot together. Dermot took a step forwards, but a gesture from Lerntowski made him stop in his tracks. Aisling struggled again, with as little success as before. John Smith struck a match and lit his pipe.

"Tell me where the machine is—or your cat will lose its head," squeaked Lerntowski coldly.

Aisling appealed to Dermot. "Can't you stop her?"

Dermot, his face grey, looked imploringly at Lerntowski. He opened his mouth to speak.

"Quiet!" Lerntowski snapped at him. Dermot flushed and turned away towards the fireplace. He grasped the mantelpiece like a drowning man a straw and waited, his back rigid.

"For the last time, where is the machine?" Lerntowski asked, as expressionlessly as before.

The window cleaner gave Aisling's arm an extra twist. The little old lady raised the knife above Mulligan's neck. Mulligan, oblivious of his impending fate, continued to purr loudly.

"No!" cried Aisling. "Let him go! I'll tell you everything."

The little old lady smiled and laid down the knife. Mulligan stood up on the back of the chair and arched himself to rub against her: was nobody ever going to finish feeding him? The little old lady stepped back a pace and fastidiously cleaned the hand which had been touching him on her skirt.

"Well?" asked Lerntowski.

"Peter has it," Aisling said reluctantly. "He's taking it to Hermann."

Lerntowski looked questioningly at John Smith.

"She spent last night with Hermann's son Peter and Margarethe Souter," said the latter calmly, puffing away at his pipe. "If she had it, she could have passed it on there."

"Where is Hermann?" asked Lerntowski. "We thought he would be here. Where has he gone to?"

Aisling hesitated.

The little old lady picked up the knife again.

"He's in Zurich," Aisling said hastily. "Hermann's holding a meeting there. But I don't know where in Zurich. Honest I don't."

Lerntowski looked at her closely. "I believe you," he said finally. He paced up and down the room. The others were silent. The only sounds were Mulligan's purring and the odd sneeze as Shavitov walked off his allergy in the snow outside.

Finally Lerntowski stopped. He spoke rapidly in the foreign language. The others nodded. He left the room, ignoring Aisling completely. She wondered anxiously what he was up to now.

Through the window she saw a black limousine drive smoothly off. It was so quiet, it was no wonder she hadn't heard it arrive. Were Shavitov and Lerntowski going to Zurich to try to find Hermann and the others? She wished she hadn't had to tell them about the meeting in Zurich, but she'd had no choice. That awful old woman would have killed Mulligan as soon as blink. All the same...

The others waited until the limousine was out of sight. Then John Smith stood up and knocked out his pipe in the hearth. Dermot went into the hall and returned with a length of rope. He tied Aisling's hands behind her back.

"Okay, Ash?" he asked softly. "Not too tight?"

She didn't answer.

"Ilse and Pat have one or two things to do, isn't that right, so you're coming with us. We're taking the taxi to visit Seamus. He'll be pleased to see you again. Come on, Mulligan. You'll be best with us, isn't that right?" He picked up the cat and led Aisling gently towards the door.

John Smith followed them. "Wait a minute," he said. "I almost forgot my encyclopedias."

Dermot steered Aisling out into the snow, opened the taxi door and helped her into the back. John Smith came out of the chalet, dumped his briefcase on the front seat and climbed in beside her. Dermot got into the driver's seat and started the engine. Mulligan stretched, yawned and then collapsed, purring, across Dermot's knees. Dermot tucked his tail out of the way of the gear lever and drove off.

Aisling looked back. There was no sign of either the window cleaner or the little old lady and the chalet looked as picturesque and peaceful as it had when she and Dermot had first arrived.

17
Prisoners

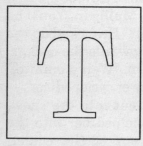hey drove along the lake for a few miles and then turned off the main road and headed towards the mountains. The scenery changed and soon they were passing though a forest of dark, snow-mantled pine trees. It was breathtakingly beautiful; if she hadn't been a prisoner, being taken to a secret destination and possibly to her death, Aisling thought she might have enjoyed the journey.

As the light began to fade in the late afternoon, snow began to fall. They were right up in the Alps now, beyond the tree line, and jagged peaks loomed eerily above them through gaps in the curtain of snow. The snow became heavier. As soon as the taxi's wipers swept a patch of windscreen clear, huge white flakes obscured it again. Dermot hunched forwards over the wheel, peering out into the swirling whiteness where the car's lights drowned in the falling snow, and muttered inaudibly to himself. Aisling sat rigid with fear, expecting them to skid over the edge of a precipice at any moment.

Only John Smith remained unperturbed. He chattered cheerfully about the weather, about the geological formation of the Alps, about the number of accidents annually on Swiss roads, about the fact that Switzerland not only had a navy and no sea, but had the largest army in Europe, and about the length of time it took a man to freeze to death. It didn't seem to bother him that neither Dermot not Aisling paid him the slightest bit of attention.

Suddenly Dermot swung the wheel to the right and drove the taxi straight into the mountainside. The tyres, despite the heavy chains around them, spun furiously on the snow, then got a grip, and Dermot urged the car forwards into what looked like a blank white swirling wall. Aisling shut her eyes. *Taxi discovered in Alpine crevasse. The skeletons of two men, a girl and a cat were stumbled upon yesterday by Swiss mountaineers...*

The taxi leapt forwards as its wheels gripped firmer ground. She dared to open her eyes again. She blinked. The wall in front of them had split apart!

Dermot jammed on the brakes and the taxi skidded to a halt, caught in a blaze of lights like a rabbit in the headlamps of a car. The lights stabbed down at them from every side. Walls of solid rock towered over them to meet in the darkness high above her head.

They were inside the mountain!

***

"Well, here we are then, isn't that right?" Dermot turned off the ignition.

"Where are we?"

John Smith sighed. "You turned down my offer of an *Encyclopedia for the Expansion of Young Minds*, didn't you?" he asked reproachfully. "If you hadn't, you'd know all about the mountains Eiger, Munch and Jungfrau and their relative heights and geographical positions. This, incidentally, is the Jungfrau or Young Lady—not very appropriate in the circumstances. And," he continued, waving aside Aisling's attempted interruption, "in Volume 10 under S for Subterranean you could have learnt all about caverns and caves, both natural and unnatural.

As you may have noticed, this one is unnatural."

Aisling wasn't surprised.

Dermot had got down from the cab and he now flung open the passenger door . "Welcome to Holiday Home, Ash! Out you come and let's see what the boss wants done with you, isn't that right?"

Aisling looked appealingly at John Smith, but he was no help. "Stand not upon your going, but go," he advised. "See Volume 9 under Q for Quotations: Shakespeare's *Macbeth*, more or less, if I'm not mistaken. Can I help you out?"

"Thank you. I can manage."

She scrambled out of the taxi (difficult enough with her hands tied behind her back) and looked around her. The cavern was immense. People were coming and going in all directions, some in white overalls, others in some kind of uniform with machine guns slung over their shoulders. Various vehicles were parked around the cavern floor: lorries, jeeps and, Aisling bit her lip, a highly-patterned tanker with PARECETALOXYDIOCLORI-NITROGLYCERSULPHIDE GAS written along its side. It was at the far end of the cavern, directly opposite them.

She started to run towards it, but Dermot

pulled her back. "You'll meet Seamus soon enough, Ash. You've got to see the boss first, isn't that right? Come on."

"On you go, Aisling," said John Smith encouragingly.

Dermot turned to him. "See you later, mate," he said. "Oh—and you'd better look after the cat. The boss'd have a fit if he knew I'd brought him, but there was no way I could leave him with that bunch of murdering so-and-sos, isn't that right? That Ilse would kill him as soon as look at him."

"You may be right." John Smith took Mulligan from Dermot and stroked him gently. "Hardly a catophile, our Frau Schultz. Look under G for Greek, Aisling: philos meaning loving. Not a word I'd apply to dear Ilse in any circumstances."

Aisling didn't reply.

***

Dermot took her through a door in the cavern wall and along a well-lit passageway hewn out of the rock. Eventually, after what seemed like miles underground, they reached another door. Dermot knocked.

The door was opened from within and

Dermot pushed her through it. She looked round. She was in an incredibly white office. The walls and ceiling were covered in some highly-polished, shining metal (no doubt John Smith would have been able to tell her what it was, she thought bitterly). The furniture was also made largely of metal and upholstered in white leather. The carpet, whose pile was so deep Aisling's shoes practically disappeared in it, stretched from wall to wall like an advertisement for washing powder. An immense desk, with an array of almost as many switches and gadgets as Seamus's console at home, took up most of the office. Behind it, dressed immaculately in a white suit, light grey shirt and black-and-white tie, sat Lerntowski.

Aisling looked for Shavitov. He had opened the door for them and was now standing behind them, waiting. He was wearing black, Aisling noticed, and was still as scruffy-looking as he'd been on the train and in Hermann's chalet. His suit looked as if it had been bought in an Oxfam shop and then slept in for a week. Shavitov didn't look too good himself, either. His eyes were red and watery and he kept sneezing surreptitiously into a large once-white handkerchief.

He glared at Aisling over the top of it. "You

hav brought zat accursed cat, no?" he asked. A huge sneeze forced its way through the handkerchief: either they'd brought some of Mulligan's hairs with them or he still hadn't recovered from his last allergic attack.

Lerntowski snapped an order and Shavitov jumped to attention. He moved away from Aisling and Dermot and stood beside the desk.

"Good evening, child," squeaked Lerntowski coldly. "It is a pleasure to have you as my guest."

Aisling said nothing.

"As you have perhaps noticed, your godfather and his sister are also paying us a visit." He smiled, showing sharp, rat-like teeth.

Aisling continued to say nothing.

"And we have sent someone to Zurich to persuade Hermann and his charming family to join us soon. In the meantime, we shall, I hope, make you comfortable. Take her to 105!"

Aisling abandoned her resolve not to talk. She didn't know what 105 was, but she didn't like the sound of it. And maybe, if she could see Seamus again, he might find a way of getting them out of here. "Can't I see Seamus and Florence first?" she asked quickly. "They're both very old, you know. And Seamus is a sick man. He could die, you realize, if you don't treat him properly."

A strange expression spread across Lerntowski's narrow face. An even stranger sound came from his lips. Aisling decided, with a shiver, that it must be laughter.

"They are both well. Too well." Lerntowski sounded bitter. "But if you want to speak to them, why not? When he knows that we have you, perhaps your godfather will be more co-operative."

Aisling regretted having spoken.

Dermot led her back along the corridor to the main cavern. Shavitov came with them. He kept the handkerchief over his nose but he couldn't help sneezing continually. Aisling found this amusing until he caught her eye; after that, she tried to look as concerned as possible.

A sort of balcony ran along the inner wall of the cavern and they walked along this towards the tanker. They stopped opposite it. The tanker stood about ten feet away, illuminated by at least four spotlights; guards with machine guns surrounded it on all sides. Obviously Florence and Seamus were still inside and had refused to come out.

Shavitov unhooked a megaphone from the railing in front of him. "You talk to grandaddy, no?" he ordered through his handkerchief.

"No," said Aisling. If she didn't talk, Seamus might think they were bluffing when they said they had her. She tried to feel brave but, with her hands tied behind her back and a sinking feeling as if she'd been torpedoed, butterflies and all, in her stomach, it wasn't easy.

Shavitov took his handkerchief away from his face. His eyes shone. His lips curved up in a smile. "You vant I hurt you a leetle, no? Because of train perhaps? Or because of cat? I enjoy to hurt you a leetle, yes?" he offered.

"I'd talk to Seamus, Ash," advised Dermot. "There's no point in getting yourself hurt, isn't that right? And you can't harm him just by talking to him."

Aisling clenched her teeth stubbornly.

Shavitov smiled again. He took up the megaphone in his huge hairy hands. "Hey, Grandaddy!" he bellowed. Daddy, addy, addy, addy... echoed across the cavern roof and around the walls. Shavitov lowered his voice a little. "Ve hav leetle girl, no? You tell leetle girl to talk to you or ve make it verry deeficult for leetle girl to talk ever again, no?"

There was a silence for a moment. Then Seamus's voice boomed out into the cavern. "Huh!" he said. Huh, uh, uh... went the echoes, one after another.

Shavitov clenched his fist on the railing. The railing, Aisling noticed, started to bend. "I am not saying ze jokes," he whispered softly into the megaphone. "I gives you one more chance, zen..."

Aisling shivered.

"All right, you oversized moron." Seamus sounded bored. "If you're there, child, you'd better say a few words. Just to keep the people happy. Recite 'Ba Ba Blacksheep' or something and then we can get back to our dinner."

A hungry feeling invaded the torpedo hole in Aisling's stomach. It had been a long time since breakfast and the thought of Florence's cooking was enough to make her feel quite faint. Dermot seemed to have had the same reaction. She heard him gulp behind her.

Shavitov held the microphone in front of her mouth. "Speak!" he ordered.

"I'm sorry." Aisling felt tears pricking her eyelids. She forced them back. "I didn't mean to get caught. I just never thought that Dermot..."

"Fiddlesticks!" interrupted Seamus. Sticks, icks, icks, icks... went the echoes. "You just never thought. Full stop. I assume that at least you had the sense to get rid of my machine before they got you. You must have done, or they wouldn't be bothering with this charade now."

"I think Hermann has it. Peter was taking it
to him." The others had got that out of her
already, she thought, and at least Seamus
knew now what the situation was.

"Good." Seamus seemed satisfied. "Now, do
you want to talk any more, or can I go back to my
food? My roast chicken's getting cold. Oh, wait
a minute. Florence wants to have a word with
you."

Aisling suddenly felt more hopeful. She
looked round the cavern, at the spotlights, the
machine guns, the guards: trust Seamus to
behave as if this was nothing more than an
ordinary telephone conversation.

There was a pause and then Florence's voice
rang out. "Are you hearing me, Aisling?" Ling,
ing, ing... rang round the cavern roof.

"Yes, thank you." Aisling couldn't help
smiling. "I'm hearing you very well. How are
you both?"

"Well, naturally. How else should we be? It's
you that I'm worried about. What would your
mother think of the way we've looked after you?
Are you at least eating properly? You're a
growing girl, remember, and you mustn't skimp
your food. Three good meals a day is what you
need and none of these convenience foods

either."

The last meal Aisling had eaten had been breakfast at Tante Margarethe's that morning. She hoped John Smith had at least fed Mulligan. "I'm all right," she said, hoping she sounded more cheerful than she felt. "And Mulligan is too."

"Good. Just remember to look after yourself."

Shavitov grabbed the megaphone. "Zees ees enough!" he shouted impatiently. Nuff, uff, uff... went the echoes. "You know now zat ze girl ees here. You come out of zat tanker or ve make it, how you say? hot for her, no?"

There was a silence from the tanker. Aisling waited nervously.

"No deal." Seamus said it quietly. "I have never given in to blackmail—shush, Florence!—and I do not intend to start now. Over and out."

The tanker was silent.

Shavitov threw down the megaphone. He took a step towards Aisling.

"Wait a minute, pal." Dermot moved between them. "The boss said to let her speak to them. He didn't say anything else, isn't that right? I'm taking her to 105 now."

Shavitov hesitated for a long, long minute. Aisling kept behind Dermot.

Shavitov stepped back and sneezed into his handkerchief again. "Okay," he snuffled through it. "But remember, girl," he shouted after them as Dermot hurried her back along the balcony, "I am not forgetting vat you hav done to me. I vill get even soon, no?"

"Not if I can help it," muttered Dermot under his breath.

Aisling stopped. "Whose side are you on? I thought you were with them."

Dermot grinned sheepishly down at her. "Me, Ash? I'm on the side that wins. But I don't like violence, isn't that right? Lerntowski has people looking for your Hermann. Let's hope they find him soon before he can get his machine working."

"But Hermann's machine is the only thing that can stop ultra-violet rays getting through the hole S.K.U.N.K. have made in the ozone layer! If he doesn't get it to work, we'll all die!"

"Not at all, Aisling. You don't think anybody's going to let it go that far, do you? Once the governments realize that nobody can stop S.K.U.N.K., they'll give them what they want and S.K.U.N.K. will let the ozone hole close again, isn't that right? Seamus has just been making things worse, meddling in matters he doesn't understand. Once Hermann's been stopped, you and Seamus and dear old Flo and Mulligan can all go home again, isn't that right? You don't belong in a nasty place like this."

"And you do?"

"I belong where there's money, Ash." Dermot held up his hand. "Now, don't you start moralizing, 'cos that won't get you anywhere. Florrie's been trying to keep me on the straight and narrow for years, isn't that right? I owe a lot to Flo; without her, I'd have been in jail a lot more often, and that's a fact. I did intend to go straight this time, too. I gave her my word." He looked worried for a moment. "But needs must and all that, isn't that right? Lerntowski made me an offer too good to refuse when he hijacked the tanker. And I'll see that no-one gets hurt, isn't that right? You can be sure of that."

Aisling wondered what chance Dermot had of stopping any of S.K.U.N.K.'s agents, especially Shavitov, from doing anything they wanted, but decided there was no point in saying so. "Where are we going to now?" she asked instead.

"I'm taking you to 105, like I was told. You can lie low there until Hermann's been found and all this kerfuffle is over and done with, isn't that right? Come on."

He led Aisling through a door in the wall of

the cavern and along another long passageway. Doors appeared in its sides, set close together and numbered consecutively. He stopped at door 105 and opened it. The room, or cell, was hardly more than a few feet in either direction. Apart from a bed, there was no furniture. The only source of light was an electric bulb hanging from the ceiling. There were no windows.

Dermot pushed her through the door. "Sorry about this, Ash. But it's not too bad, really. And I think you'll be safest here, isn't that right? There's a blanket on the bed in case you're cold and I'll send someone down with some food as soon as I can. Here, I'll take that off." He cut through the rope round her wrists. "There's no need to have you tied up in here, isn't that right? There's enough room to exercise. You should do press-ups and knee-bends and maybe a bit of running on the spot. Think of it as an opportunity to get fit, isn't that right? And I'll see you later."

The door clanged, a key turned in the lock, footsteps sounded fainter and fainter down the passage, and Aisling was left alone.

18
Escape

ours passed, maybe days.
Aisling looked at her
watch: twenty minutes
since Dermot had left her. She got up from the
bed and started to pace the length of the cell.
Five steps to the opposite wall, five steps back
again. One of her paces would be about two feet,
she calculated, so that would be twenty feet.
Twenty feet to the wall and back. And how
many feet in a mile? Her father had muttered
on once about some crazy number of yards in a
mile, hadn't he? She tried to remember. Rats.
Okay, so she'd have to convert her paces into
metres. A metre is longer than a yard and
twenty feet is six yards and a bit, so say six
metres to the wall and back. Six into a
thousand. She did a quick sum in the dust on
the floor of the cell: one hundred and sixty six

times. And that was only a kilometre. Which was what? Five eighths of a mile? So say about three hundred times to the mile. Three hundred times!

She looked at her watch again. Only half an hour since Dermot had left. She sighed, pulled the cuff of her anorak down over her wrist so that she wouldn't be tempted to keep looking at the time, stood up and started walking. It was very boring. Five steps to the wall, five back to the door; five steps to the wall, five back to the door... Her head began to spin. She threw herself down on the bed and stared up at the ceiling.

Suddenly footsteps sounded outside in the passage. There was a scuffle, a clanging noise, someone swore. The lock grated, the handle turned and the door swung open.

"Will you get out from under my feet you gluttonous, greedy, voracious, ravenous, overfed, overgorged, overindulged, importuning, pestering, plaguish feline?" John Smith stood in the doorway with his briefcase in one hand and a tray in the other. Mulligan was performing a figure of eight around his ankles. As John Smith stepped over him, a metal bowl on the tray slid sideways and crashed into a metal plate with the clanging sound Aisling had heard.

"Here you are then, Aisling. Room service." He passed her the tray over Mulligan's head. Mulligan jumped onto the bed and curved a paw towards the food on the plate.

"You wouldn't believe I fed him in the kitchen. Here, boy. You come and try this and let Aisling eat in peace." He took a bar of chocolate from his pocket. Mulligan lost interest in Aisling's supper, plunged off the bed, balanced on his hindquarters and begged.

"Bon appetit, Aisling. Eat up while I keep this glutton (see under G for Greed, Volume 4) occupied."

Aisling attacked the food on the tray with only slightly less greed than Mulligan was demonstrating. Perhaps it wasn't up to Florence's standard, but to someone who hadn't eaten for over twelve hours, it tasted like manna from heaven.

"Finished? I'll take the tray back then. You might as well keep the cat. The cook was threatening to turn him into Irish stew before I lured him down here. Personally, I think he'd be pretty inedible, which comes, as you no doubt know, from the Latin *edere* to eat and the prefix *in* meaning not, see Volume 6 under L. Take care of yourself, as Florence would say."

He threw Aisling the remains of the chocolate bar and turned to leave.

"But... Aren't you going to...? Why...? What...?"

"Sorry, but much as I'd love to have a philosophical discussion with you, I have to go. They're waiting for me upstairs. I'll leave a few sample encyclopedias with you. They may help to pass the time and will certainly improve your mind." He put the briefcase on the bed. The door clanged to behind him.

Aisling felt even worse than she'd done before. Her hopes had risen when John Smith arrived, but now they were dashed again: she'd been crazy to think, even for a moment, that he wasn't really working for the enemy. There was absolutely nobody who could help her. She remembered Shavitov's threats and shivered. *Intrepid schoolgirl outwits international gang!* Some chance, she thought bitterly.

She looked at the remains of the chocolate on the bed where John Smith had thrown it. I suppose I ought to keep that for emergencies, she thought. Mulligan, sitting upright on the floor, was eyeing it too. What the heck. She ate a square of chocolate and gave Mulligan the rest. He licked the floor carefully to make sure no crumbs were being wasted, then jumped up onto her knees, wound his tail round his nose and started to purr gently. She remembered reading somewhere that people who keep cats have fewer heart attacks and nervous breakdowns than people who don't: certainly, having Mulligan curled up affectionately on her, quite unworried about the future, gave her a great deal of comfort.

She stroked the cat absently and wondered what to do now. She supposed she might as well look at the encyclopedias John Smith had left: even reading an encyclopedia would be better than walking up and down like a caged animal or driving herself insane worrying about what was going to happen to her and to Florence and Seamus. She doubted very much if S.K.U.N.K. would let them go once they'd destroyed Hermann's machine, despite what Dermot had said.

She opened the briefcase. There wasn't a single encyclopedia in it!

She shook her head and looked again. A well-sealed parcel lay at the foot of the case, on top of it was a small square box and on top of the box was a piece of white card. This had AISLING written on it. And sellotaped to the card was a key.

She picked up the card and turned it over. On

the other side was written:

> BEWARE MICROPHONES! Go at 9.55
> exactly. Leave bag in cell and lock it in. DO
> NOT, repeat NOT, TOUCH BOX! Follow
> corridor to your right. Go straight until
> you reach the door, then wait.

She forced herself to sit still. So John Smith was
on their side after all! And he had rescued her
from Shavitov and Lerntowski in Dalkey. Had
he hoped to save her in Thun too? She wondered
how he had convinced Lerntowski that he was
working for S.K.U.N.K. Most of all, she
wondered what was in the box.

She bent down and listened. It made a very
faint but very definite ticking sound. She
wasn't really surprised, she realized. Very, very
carefully, she put the briefcase on the floor. She
looked at her watch: 9.10. Only 45 minutes to
wait. She thought of all the poetry she knew:
Yeats's "Innisfree"; Kipling's "If";
Wordsworth's "Daffodils"; "Hickory, dickory,
dock"... only that reminded her of clocks and
she didn't particularly want to think about
them at the moment. She looked at her watch
again: 9.29. She tried to remember the chemical
symbols for all the metals; she struggled

haphazardly through all the history dates she could think of; she said her multiplication tables from one to twelve and back down to one again... 9.43.

Finally, it was 9.55.

Picking up Mulligan and placing him over her shoulder, she tiptoed to the door. She slid the key into the lock and turned it as quietly as possible. She eased the door open.

There was no-one in the corridor.

She locked the door as she'd been ordered, hoping that John Smith's watch agreed with hers and that she had time to get well away before whatever was in the small square box did what she feared it was going to do, and tiptoed along the passageway. It was a long way to the door but she met no-one. The door wasn't quite closed and a thin ribbon of light crept round its edge. Aisling peeked through the gap.

Ahead of her she saw the cavern. It was quieter now, but people were still moving about and the noise of machinery was still evident. The tanker was directly opposite her, at the far side of the cavern, so she reasoned she must be near the entrance. To her left was a kind of control box, like a signal box on a railway. She could see a man inside it, poring over a series of dials and flashing lights.

As she watched, the door of the box opened quietly and a dark figure entered. She held her breath. The figure raised his hand and brought it down sharply across the controller's neck. The controller slumped forwards. The figure turned round and looked towards her. It was John Smith. She started to open the door, but he held up his hand warningly. "Wait!" he mouthed. She took a firm grip on Mulligan and stayed where she was.

John Smith flicked a switch. The cavern was plunged into darkness. A groaning, creaking sound came from the wall beyond the control box. The darkness split and stars appeared. Inside the cavern, confusion reigned. People shouted. An engine sprang to life. Gunfire echoed round the cavern roof like thunder.

"Come on, Aisling!" yelled John Smith. "Now!"

He grabbed her and rushed towards the opening in the wall. A huge vehicle raced towards them, threatening to crush them in its path. It skidded to a halt beside them and Aisling, bemused, realized that it was the tanker. Shots ricocheted off it as John Smith opened the passenger door, pushed her and Mulligan up and climbed in behind them.

The tanker raced through the gap in the wall

and out into the clear night air. Its wheels skidded dangerously on the fresh snow and it careered towards the precipice, but Florence, seated at the wheel, remained unruffled. She turned the wheel calmly into the skid, avoided the precipice by inches and steered the tanker back onto the mountain road.

"I didn't know you could dr..." Aisling started. She was interrupted by an immense explosion behind them. She looked back. The whole side of the mountain appeared to have blown out and sparks were shooting into the air like a manic firework display. The snow-covered mountain tops were illuminated for a minute by a brilliant red glare as a second huge explosion occurred.

"The fuel depot," said John Smith. "I hoped as much."

"Well done!" Florence leant across Aisling and squeezed his hand.

"Stop messing about, woman, and concentrate on the driving. We haven't got all day!" Seamus was obviously alive and well in the bed behind them.

"Backseat drivers," muttered Florence. She put her foot down hard on the accelerator. Aisling grabbed the edge of the seat and wished she were more religious: if ever St Christopher was needed to protect travellers, it was now, she thought, as they sped back down the precipitous mountain road, skidding round hairpin bends, bumping off frozen walls of snow, even turning through a complete circle at one stage when they hit a patch of black ice.

Somehow, they reached the valley floor all in one piece. Aisling still didn't feel safe, though. They were on the motorway now, and Florence continued to drive the tanker as if it were a Ferrari, veering from lane to lane to overtake everything on the road.

"Where did you learn to drive?" she asked.

"I was driving long before you were thought of, child. I remember, back in 1952," she crossed to the inside lane to overtake a Mercedes and swung back into the fast lane again, "when Margarethe and I won the Monte Carlo Rally together. Now, that was some driving."

Aisling realized what Florence's driving had reminded her of: "Do you mean Peter's Tante Margarethe?" she asked.

"Naturally. Who else? Now, go to sleep, child. I don't know what your parents would say if they knew Seamus was keeping you up like this. I'm sure it's long past your bedtime."

"That's right, woman," Seamus grunted over the intercom. "Blame it on me. Losing a bit of sleep never hurt anyone yet."

Aisling grinned. If her parents had the slightest idea of all the things that had happened to her since she'd left home, they'd have had a heart attack by now. At the very least. Before she took Florence's advice, however, there was something she had to clear up. She turned to John Smith. "Who are you?"

"Me?" John Smith raised an eyebrow. "I'm an encyclopedia salesman. Didn't I tell you? Though in my spare time, I must admit, I work for MI5, which, as the *Encyclopedia for the Expansion of Young Minds* would readily inform you, is the eyes and ears of the British Government, bless its purple socks."

"MI5!" Aisling couldn't believe her ears. "That's spies and everything! What were you doing in Ireland?"

A snort came through the intercom. "Just what I was about to ask myself. I had thought that even the British had finally caught up with the fact that we became self-governing in 1922. What is MI5 doing interfering in our internal affairs?"

"It's alright, Grandad. Calm down." Aisling had to smother a fit of the giggles as Seamus almost choked with indignation in the back. "I was there at the request of your own government. S.K.U.N.K. is nobody's internal affair. They are out to wreck the world."

"You saved me from Shavitov and Lerntowski back in Dalkey, didn't you? How on earth did you get Lerntowski to trust you after that?"

"My innate charm, Aisling. What else? Together with an immutable (we don't have a dictionary for you to check and the encyclopedias are sacrificed to a nobler cause, so I shall tell you, free, gratis and for nothing, that that means unchangeable; don't bother to thank me) belief on the part of our friend Lerntowski, that everyone is as corrupt as himself. I just had to spin a convincing story."

"That shouldn't have been too difficult," Seamus muttered grumpily through the intercom.

"Are S.K.U.N.K. all dead?" Aisling asked. "And Dermot too?" She thought how nice he had been to Mulligan (and to herself, when he could) even though he'd gone over to the enemy's side. She didn't want to hear that he'd been blown up with Shavitov and Lerntowski and the others.

John Smith looked serious. "I know, Aisling. I quite liked that young man as well. But, if you will play with fire... Maybe those who were deep underground escaped, I don't know. But I do know that their laboratory has been destroyed. That at least has been achieved."

"Oh. Does that mean that the ozone layer's all right again now?"

"Does that mean that the ozone layer's all right again now?" Seamus mimicked over the intercom. "The universe doesn't work on the same principle as instant coffee, child."

"You know what I mean," Aisling appealed to John Smith.

"S.K.U.N.K. can do no further damage to it now, so it shouldn't get worse. But the ozone may take a long time to regenerate itself: *re* again, *generare* to beget, as the encyclopedia would inform you instantly."

"You mean, it'll take some time to close up again?"

"Exactly."

"We're going to Zurich now, aren't we? If Hermann's put his machine together and S.K.U.N.K. haven't got to it yet, then it should be able to close up the hole much more quickly, shouldn't it?"

"That's a question for Seamus, I fear. He's the scientific genius."

"Hmpf," came from the back of the tanker.

"Well?" Aisling asked over the intercom. "Will Hermann's machine be able to close the hole?"

"My component will work. I don't know about all the others."

John Smith grinned. "We'll just have to wait and see, Aisling. At least, at the rate Florence is driving, we shouldn't have to wait all that much longer. I'm beginning to wish I sold life-insurance instead of encyclopedias."

Florence swung the wheel to overtake a BMW on the inside. "Don't be impertinent, young man."

Aisling settled herself back on the seat and closed her eyes. "Well, even if it does take some time, at least the world is saved," she said sleepily.

She heard Seamus's answer just before she fell asleep. "The world is never saved, child," he muttered grumpily. "People are much too stupid for that. As soon as one danger is averted, they'll invent another. Don't raise your hopes."

19
Zurich

isling opened her eyes. They were crossing a bridge, she realized. The street lamps threw quivering aureoles of light onto the black water beneath; ahead, a cathedral stood floodlit, its twin towers topped by small domes which glowed like polished gold against the black of the night sky. They passed a blue single-decker tram and turned into a narrow alleyway. Florence pulled up on a thick carpet of snow. "This is the place, isn't it?" she asked quietly over the intercom.

"This is it," Seamus agreed equally quietly from behind them. "It's the end house, the one with the balcony on the first floor. Do you see any S.K.U.N.K. men about?"

"Not so's you'd notice," said John Smith. "But there could be. Shall I go and have a look?"

He opened the door. Nothing moved in the alley. He jumped down onto the snow and waited. Still nothing moved. He walked as far as the end house, looking into each doorway as he passed. Then, with a glance up at the closed shutters above him, he came back. "All clear," he reported.

"Fine. Now, I want Florence to park this confounded vehicle across the street. Only do it quietly, woman. We don't want anyone to know we're here yet, just in case S.K.U.N.K. have got here first. "

Florence eased the tanker into reverse and backed it at an angle across the road. The gears clashed and Seamus swore violently. Florence glanced at Aisling, pursed her lips and switched off the intercom. Aisling looked at the end house: the shutters remained closed and nobody appeared to have heard.

When the tanker was finally where Florence wanted it, parked directly across the entrance to the cul de sac so that no one could get in or out, she switched on the intercom again.

"Women drivers," Seamus growled. "Let's hope you don't make such a mess of the next operation. You'll have to get into the house without being seen and find out if we've beaten S.K.U.N.K. to it. I'll guard this exit. If you're not out in ten minutes, I'll assume the worst and sound the alarm. That ought to bring every policeman in Zurich here at the double: there's nothing the Swiss like less than someone making a noise in the middle of the night. Unless it's untidy parking or people filling in their forms wrong. Come on, then! Get a move on! We haven't got all night! I, for one, want to go home. "

John Smith grinned at Florence, jumped out of the tanker and helped her down. Aisling followed them along the narrow alley. John Smith had a pistol in his hand and Florence had her crossbow at the ready. Aisling wished she had some sort of weapon too. Perhaps she should have stayed in the tanker with Seamus—but it was too late now. *Schoolgirl helps foil dangerous gang of international criminals!* she thought, trying to raise her spirits. But it might too easily turn into *Schoolgirl shot in Zurich massacre.* Butterflies, bearing lumps of lead, winged back to her stomach again.

They reached the door. It was locked. John Smith felt in his pocket and brought out a set of keys. The second one fitted the lock. He pushed the door open quietly and Florence and Aisling followed him inside. They found themselves in a spacious entrance hall. The rooms on either side were dark and empty. They climbed the stairs to the first floor as quietly as possible. There was no one on the landing. A double door faced them across the polished floorboards. To their right, French windows, now shuttered, led onto the balcony.

John Smith tiptoed over to the door and put his ear to the keyhole. He beckoned to Aisling and Florence. Aisling looked through a crack at the edge of the door. Peter, five men and a woman were sitting round a table in the centre of the room. The man at the head of the table was facing the door, so Aisling could see him clearly. He was a big man, even sitting down, but unlike Shavitov, his bulk was composed of muscle rather than fat. He had short curly brown hair and a curly brown beard and his face, though at the moment expressing anger and impatience, gave Aisling a warm feeling of confidence. Peter sat next to him and she guessed that the man must be his father, Hermann. So the other five must be the other inventors, she thought. One of the men was obviously oriental—Chinese most likely—and another, small and swarthy, was probably South American. The African scientist sat on Peter's left and beside him was a tall slim man with fairish hair. A small, vivacious-looking woman with long red hair and an emerald green suit made up the complement.

Hermann was speaking to someone Aisling couldn't see. "This is pointless," he said calmly. "Nobody is going to tell you anything."

A voice Aisling knew only too well answered from the other side of the door. "Be silent!" ordered Frau Schultz, the little old lady. "I hav varned you already. If you do not be silent, ve shoot."

Hermann shrugged.

"Your boss has had plenty of time to get here," said the Chinese-looking gentleman quietly. "He is not coming."

"Call it a day, guys," suggested the small, swarthy man in a lazy drawl. (She'd been wrong: he must be the North American scientist, Aisling thought.) "Just give up and go home."

"Shut up, all of yez!" snapped another familiar voice. The window cleaner was in the room as well. "Amn't I just after telling you? The boss is on his way. He'll make you talk. He'll find out where you've hid your prize machine and he'll smash it into pieces smaller than a gnat's elbow, so he will. Then we'll see who's won!"

John Smith touched Aisling's arm and motioned her away from the door. "Did you hear that?" he whispered.

"They haven't found the machine yet and they're expecting Lerntowski to come. They don't know that we've destroyed S.K.U.N.K.'s lab and blown up all the rest of the gang as well."

Aisling felt a great deal of satisfaction as she imagined the window cleaner's face when he found out the truth. "They're going to get a terrible shock!"

John Smith smiled at her. "They will indeed. But when? That, as Shakespeare (whom I'm sure you don't need to look up) would say, is the question."

Aisling stared at him. "Now, of course. We've got to rescue the people in there. There's three of us and only two of them, after all."

"We only heard two of them," Florence corrected gently. "And, even if you're right, Aisling, both of them must be armed. And there are seven innocent people right in the line of fire. We have to disarm Ilse and that man without anyone getting hurt."

"Can't we rush them?" Aisling suggested.

"Too risky," said John Smith. "We might get Pat, but Ilse would have time to shoot. We need to distract their attention."

"The balcony!" Florence opened the French windows to the right of the stairs and pushed back the heavy wooden shutters. Sure enough, they led onto the balcony which ran along the front of the house.

"Out you go, Aisling," she said. "When you get to the next window, crouch down under the sill and rap on the shutters. Remember to crouch down, now; I don't want to have to return you to your parents full of holes. I feel we haven't been looking after you properly as it is. I'm sure you've lost weight and you're looking very peaky. "

"I'm fine, really I am." Aisling stepped through the French windows. Beneath her she could see the alley with the tanker parked across it. She waved, but there was no answering sign from the tanker. She crept stealthily to the next window. Inside the room she could hear people speaking again.

"Vere hav you hidden ze machine?" the little old lady was asking angrily. "You vill tell us before ze ozzers get here. Vere is it?"

"Go look up a gum tree, you old hag!" said a woman's voice with an Australian accent.

Without waiting to hear more, Aisling rapped loudly on the shutters.

"Vat vas zat?" asked the little old lady sharply.

"What?" came the window cleaner's voice, edgy and abrupt.

Aisling rapped again: Da-di-di-da-da-da-da!

She ducked just in time. A shower of machine gun bullets came through the window, shattering the glass and splintering the shutters.

A second later, Seamus sounded the tanker's alarm. It wasn't quite as ear-shattering as it had been in the confined space of the ship's hold, but it resounded across the snow-covered city loudly enough to wake a flock of roosting starlings on a nearby church and make them scatter into the air in a black shrieking wheeling crowd. In the distance a police siren started up. Aisling hoped they would get here soon.

One of the bullets had hit the catch on the shutters and the two halves now swung open, revealing the broken window and the room inside. Cautiously, she looked into the room. The window cleaner was lying on the floor, either dead or unconscious. As she watched, John Smith bent over him and picked up his machine gun. Florence was standing next to the little old lady, her crossbow touching the latter's scrawny neck. "Drop it, Ilse," she said.

The little old lady, her face twisted with rage, dropped the machine gun she was holding. Florence kicked it demurely towards the group at the table who were sitting open-mouthed and staring.

The American picked it up and put it on the table in front of him. "Florence!" he said. "I sure am glad to see you!"

"Good evening, Cornelius." Florence smiled at the people at the table. "And Mathilda, Lutombe, Pedro and Ho. How nice to meet you all again. And Hermann and Peter too, of course. We really must try to see each other more often."

The people at the table relaxed, smiled, stood up, grinned at Florence, grinned at John Smith, clasped each other round the shoulders and sat down again.

"Thank goodness that is all over," said the South American. "I am getting too old for this sort of thing."

"Too right, Pedro," said the Australian lady. "I must say, I'll be glad to get back home. I have work to do."

Behind Aisling, down in the alley, two police cars arrived, their sirens wailing, their blue lights flashing eerily on the snow. The cars stopped, the sirens stopped, the blue lights stopped, but the alarm bell from the tanker continued. She grinned as four policemen got out of the cars and ran to the tanker. One climbed into the cab. The alarm still continued. A second one joined him. Two minutes later, they both got out. The four men walked round the tanker, looking worried. Seamus must be amused, she thought.

She turned back to the window to say to Florence that she was going down to tell Seamus to shut off the alarm. Her mouth fell open. She dodged back under the sill again, her heart thudding against her ribs: Lerntowski was in the room with a gun in his hand.

The tables had been turned completely and S.K.U.N.K. was in command once more.

***

"Put down that crossbow," she heard Lerntowski squeak. "And you! Keep your hands on your head. Ilse, pick up your weapon and keep them covered."

Staying well back from the light, Aisling dared to peek in again. Lerntowski was facing the table and Shavitov was standing behind John Smith, his gun pressed into the latter's back. Florence sat down beside Peter at the table.

"Now," squeaked Lerntowski. "Where is your machine?"

"It isn't here," said Hermann calmly.

"Where is it? I demand to know where it is!"

The people at the table remained silent.

"It's pointless, you realize." John Smith spoke calmly in his usual conversational tone. "Your mountain's been blown up. All your equipment is destroyed. Even if you smash up Hermann's machine, the hole will close up eventually by itself."

"You think so?" Lerntowski sneered. "I shall destroy this precious machine. And then I shall rebuild my laboratory and start again. Your treachery has gained the world a reprieve, that is all. You!" he pointed at the red-haired woman. "Tell me where the machine is hidden!"

"Go jump in a billabong!"

"All right. If you will not be reasonable..." Aisling shivered at the menace in his voice. "That noise outside will bring the police at any moment. You know that, but so do I. So I am not going to waste time. Tell me where your machine is, or I shall have Shavitov kill you, one by one. Starting with the boy. Stand up, you!"

Aisling didn't wait to hear more. She ran to

the balcony rail. The police were still at the tanker. She looked down. The ground seemed a long way off. She jumped.

Fortunately she landed in a pile of soft snow. She picked herself up and raced towards the tanker. She grabbed the arm of one of the policemen. "Hurry! Please hurry! They're going to shoot Peter!"

The policeman looked at her curiously. He took out a notebook. "You are English?" he asked.

"Irish. But it doesn't matter. Come on!"

"Your name?" asked the policeman.

"They have hostages in there!" Aisling pointed desperately towards the house at the end of the alley. Light streamed out through the open shutters of the first floor room, but they were too far away to see inside.

"Do you know anything about this vehicle? It is causing a disturbance."

"S.K.U.N.K. are in that house back there!" Aisling said frantically. "They are going to shoot people! Can't you understand? Somebody is going to be shot!"

A burst of machine gun fire from the house convinced the policeman. He rapped out an order. Taking out their guns, the four policemen ran towards the house.

"Wait!" Aisling had a sudden thought. She grabbed the last policeman. "There must be a back door," she said urgently. "They must have come in by a back door."

The policeman hesitated, then he said something into his radio. "Come!" he ordered Aisling.

As she squeezed past the front end of the tanker, an object attempted to wrap itself round her ankles: Mulligan. He must have got out of the cab while the policemen were examining it. She picked him up and carried him with her to the police car. The policeman backed into the main street, turned right at the first intersection and then swerved right again into a tiny lane.

They stopped behind a large white Mercedes. Two more police cars appeared almost immediately and drew up beside them. Aisling's policeman said something to the others and led them into the middle house. Aisling followed them in; no one had told her to stay in the car, after all. And Mulligan followed Aisling. Having found her, he didn't intend to lose her again: she might, after all, be heading for something to eat.

They went through a narrow passageway, up a flight of stairs and onto an equally narrow landing. The policemen spread out on the landing and surveyed the three doors in front of them. Aisling's policeman turned round. "Which one?" he asked.

"I don't know," she whispered back.

The handle of the middle door turned. Two policemen jumped to one side of it. Aisling's policeman pulled her quickly to the other side. The rest of them pressed themselves against the banisters and waited, their guns at the ready. The door opened a crack. The policemen tensed. The door opened wider and Peter appeared in the gap.

"Don't shoot!" shouted Aisling. "It's Peter!"

The policemen froze.

Aisling's heart lightened. She had been sure the machine gun fire she'd heard earlier had been aimed at him. She waited for him to come through the door. He didn't move. His head was held up defiantly, but his face was deadly white.

Aisling was just about to run forwards when Lerntowski's voice came from behind the door. "Stand back, all of you! We have hostages and we will not hesitate to shoot. One false move and the boy is dead. Do you understand?"

The policemen looked at each other. "We understand," said Aisling's policeman. "What do you want?"

"Safe conduct to our car and then to the airport. We have a plane waiting for us there."

There was a pause. Aisling stared in anguish at Peter. He was only a couple of feet away. If she could pull him round the door quickly enough, Lerntowski mightn't have time to shoot. No, she thought. It was too risky.

The policemen obviously thought so too. "All right," said Aisling's policeman. "We agree. Stand back, men."

Peter came through the door with Lerntowski close behind him, his gun pushed into the small of Peter's back. Then came Florence in front of the little old woman, Ilse Schultz. And last of all came Hermann followed by Shavitov. The policemen stood impotently aside and let them pass.

They walked down the narrow stairs slowly, in single file. Aisling was horrified to see them getting away: if only the tanker were parked across this doorway instead of uselessly blocking the front entrance.

A man came out of the shadows at the foot of the stairs. It was Dermot.

"Hi, boss," he said cheerfully. "It seems we got company, isn't that right? Just as well I went for a jog outside instead of waiting in the car. Seems I got back just in time, isn't that right?"

At the top of the stairs, Mulligan heard Dermot's voice. He gave a prriaou! of delight. Abandoning Aisling, he raced downstairs, an orange thunderbolt, not caring who he knocked over in the process, and threw himself at Dermot, clawing his way up the latter's sweatshirt to rub his head ecstatically against his chin.

The stairs were a shambles. Shavitov, coughing and sneezing, had been knocked onto Hermann who, in turn, had been flung onto Ilse who, firing her machine gun wildly at the wall, had tumbled onto Florence and the whole lot of them had collapsed on top of Lerntowski and Peter.

Aisling raced downstairs with the policemen. Dermot stood watching, calmly stroking Mulligan behind the ears, until a policeman brought both his hands behind his back and snapped a pair of handcuffs on them.

He caught sight of Aisling. "Hiya, Ash! The game's up, isn't that right? I ought to have stayed on the side of the law, as Florence was always telling me. Are you sure you're not hurt, Flo? You took a nasty tumble there."

"I'm fine." Florence picked herself up and patted her curls back into place. "But no thanks to you. Really, Dermot, I'm disappointed in you. I thought, this time, you had really decided to turn over a new leaf and lead an honest life."

"Sorry, Flo." He smiled at her. The policeman tugged at his arm. "Come and visit me in prison. You might convert me yet, isn't that right? And look after the cat."

Florence kissed Dermot briskly on the cheek and removed Mulligan from his shoulder. "Take care," she said. "And look after yourself."

"Bless you, Flo."

"There's one more," Aisling said urgently to the policeman next to her. "There was another one upstairs."

The policeman ran upstairs and she followed him. They went through the door into a small room with another door at the far end of it. Somebody was rattling the door handle.

"Stand back!" shouted the policeman. He aimed his gun at the lock and fired. "Come through with your hands up!" he shouted.

A burly police officer came through the door. Aisling's policeman grinned sheepishly. He said something in Swiss German. The officer replied abruptly in the same language. "Come through," he said to Aisling. "Your friends are here."

She went into the room she had seen from the

balcony. The foreign scientists were still there, talking to what seemed like a hundred policemen. John Smith saw her and came over. "Thank goodness you're all right, Aisling," he said. "What happened to the others? I heard shooting. Are they okay?"

Aisling told him what had happened on the stairs. John Smith laughed. "Good old Mulligan! I always had a soft spot for that cat. They ought to make a whole new entry in the encyclopedia just for him: *felix Mulliganiensis*: the cat that saved the world!"

"What happened here?" Aisling asked. "I heard machine gun fire. I thought they'd shot Peter."

"They nearly did. Look at that table there." Long splinters of wood had been scarred from its surface. "Hermann started to tell them where the machine was when Lerntowski threatened to shoot Peter. I don't know if he was telling the truth, but he was certainly stalling for time. He must have known that the police would come at any minute. Dear Ilse thought he was stalling too. That," John Smith pointed at the table, "was her way of telling him to hurry up."

"Well, at least it convinced the police that I was serious." She looked round. The window

cleaner was still lying where he'd fallen when
John Smith attacked him.

"Is he...?"

"Come on," said John Smith. "Let's find the
others."

Epilogue

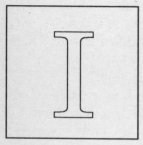t was morning by the time everybody had been taken to Zurich police station, made their statements and been allowed to go.

Aisling, John Smith and Florence returned to the tanker, where they found Seamus sitting up in bed, fuming with impatience. A mountain of angry-looking sketches of men with machine guns, women with crossbows, policemen, gallows and coffins covered most of the duvet.

"About time too!" he exploded. "I wondered when anybody would remember an old useless cripple and have the courtesy to tell him what is going on! I take it, from the complacent grins on your faces, that you have finally managed to sort S.K.U.N.K. out and get them locked up and out of harm's way. You certainly took long enough about it. Good. I'm delighted to hear it. Now, if none of you have any objections, I am going home."

"Aren't we going to stay until Hermann tests the machine?" Aisling asked.

"Why? If it works, it works. If it doesn't, we'll all have to put on sun-tan lotion and wait a little longer."

"But he might need your help."

"Rubbish. Ho and Mathilda and the others are all good scientists. They don't need me either. I suggest Mr Smith turns this glorified sardine tin round and gets us out of here."

Sure, Grandad," said John Smith cheerfully. "I'll get started immediately. Dublin, here we come!"

He jumped out of the tanker, slammed the door behind him and a couple of minutes later they heard him climb into the cab and the engine cough into life.

Seamus continued to stare grumpily in front of him as the tanker drove off. "I don't know why I bother living," he said to no one in particular. "I missed all the fun. They should shoot old people like horses when they get past it, instead of just ignoring them. Even Mulligan saw more of the action than I did."

Mulligan, hearing his name, looked up from

the armchair where he'd been sprawling comfortably. At the police station he had had an excellent meal of Swiss sausage washed down by two saucers of Swiss cream and was feeling sleek and contented. Assuming that Seamus wanted his company, he launched himself towards the bed, almost missed, clawed himself onto the duvet, knocked a dozen sketches onto the carpet and snuggled down under Seamus's chin.

Seamus made no effort to push him away. He shut his eyes. His face looked thin and tired on the pillow. For the first time, Aisling thought he actually looked like a frail old man.

Florence had been listening to him from the kitchen where she was preparing breakfast. She came through, wiping her hands on her pinny, and looked at him gravely. Then she smiled. "I quite agree," she said briskly. "You are getting past it."

Aisling was amazed. She wondered if she'd heard properly.

"It's just as well you were forced to stay out of things." Florence continued to smile sweetly. "You've had far too much excitement this trip as it is. In future, I suggest you stay at home and let someone younger do whatever's necessary."

Seamus sat up as if he'd been electrocuted.

Mulligan fell off the bed, looked surprised, stretched out full length amongst the sketches on the carpet and went back to sleep.

"Fiddlesticks, woman!" Seamus was suddenly his old self again. "Me too old? You must be mad!"

Florence winked at Aisling. "You think about it," she said. "But first, we're going to eat. A decent meal will make us all feel better." She whistled into the intercom. "Breakfast is ready, Mr Smith. I suggest you pull up and come and join us."

Breakfast lived up to Florence's usual fantastic standard. She had cooked steak and chops and bacon and liver and sausages and tomatoes and chips. Aisling hadn't had so much food for days. Not since they'd stopped in Châlons-sur-Marne, she thought, when Dermot was too drugged to drive the tanker.

"That reminds me," she said. "There's one thing I don't understand. When did Dermot change sides? Or was he working for S.K.U.N.K. right from the beginning?"

Florence sighed. "Poor Dermot."

"Poor Dermot my eye!" snorted Seamus. "I told you you were taking a chance to trust that young man."

"He *was* going straight," Florence insisted.

"If Mr Smith hadn't driven the tanker right into a S.K.U.N.K. ambush so that that horrible Lerntowski was able to bribe him, he'd have been fine."

John Smith looked down at his plate and busied himself chasing a piece of tomato onto his fork.

Aisling stared at him. "You let S.K.U.N.K. capture the tanker?"

He looked embarrassed. "Well, yes, Aisling. You see, I had to convince Lerntowski I was working for S.K.U.N.K. so that he'd take me to their headquarters. I knew you'd got Seamus's part of the machine away safely so they wouldn't get their hands on it. What I didn't know was that Dermot was such a weak character. It's a pity; I liked the lad."

"I'm sure, this time, he's learnt his lesson," Florence said briskly. "When we get home I shall see that he's extradited back to Ireland and go and visit him again. All he needs is a fresh start."

"Hmpf!" snorted Seamus.

"When will we be home?" Aisling asked.

"Not soon enough," sniffed Seamus. "Never, if we keep stopping like this for meals every five minutes."

John Smith grinned and stood up. "Message

received and understood. We'll be home tomorrow, Aisling. With a bit of luck, we should manage to catch the evening boat. Fasten your seatbelts, ladies and gentlemen: I'll see if I can emulate (*copy*, for those with neither a dictionary nor an encyclopedia) the driving of Florence and Peter's speed-crazy aunt."

***

As they hurtled back across Switzerland to the French border, Aisling thought of all the things that had happened to her since she had gone up to see Seamus in Dalkey that first day. It had certainly been worth missing hockey for. She wondered if Louise and the others would ever believe her. She wondered what her parents would say. Most of all, she wondered if she'd still have a place on the school hockey team when she got home.

Published by Poolbeg